## "I'm a ninja!"

She frantically shook her head, disbelief washing over her again as the scenario replayed through her brain. She'd assaulted a man with a jack! Yes, he'd come at her first...but she hadn't even hesitated. What had she done?

"Grace," Hollis said in a calming but wary tone, his gaze giving the strength she needed. "I need you to breathe, honey." He pushed a mass of wet hair from her face and tipped her chin up so he could look into her eyes.

His voice soothed her. His touch eased her knotted muscles as she followed his instructions. Slowly she gained her wits, until finally the hysteria passed and she could think rationally. "Hollis, two Latino men pulled up behind me on the highway. My tire blew. I'm pretty sure they set it up." She told him what had happened next and how she'd single-handedly put them on the ground. She collapsed into his powerful arms.

Hollis held her tighter and she melded into him—a safe place. The safest place she'd been since she'd lost her memory...possibly ever. She peered into his dark eyes, searching for wisdom, answers...hope.

**Jessica R. Patch** lives in the Mid-South, where she pens inspirational contemporary romance and romantic suspense novels. When she's not hunched over her laptop or going on adventurous trips with willing friends in the name of research, you can find her watching way too much Netflix with her family and collecting recipes for amazing dishes she'll probably never cook. To learn more about Jessica, please visit her at jessicarpatch.com.

### Books by Jessica R. Patch

#### Love Inspired Suspense

*Fatal Reunion*
*Protective Duty*
*Concealed Identity*
*Final Verdict*
*Cold Case Christmas*
*Killer Exposure*
*Recovered Secrets*

#### The Security Specialists

*Deep Waters*
*Secret Service Setup*
*Dangerous Obsession*

Visit the Author Profile page at Harlequin.com.

# RECOVERED SECRETS

## JESSICA R. PATCH

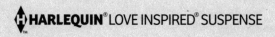
**HARLEQUIN**® LOVE INSPIRED® SUSPENSE

 LOVE INSPIRED BOOKS

ISBN-13: 978-1-335-23235-9

Recovered Secrets

Copyright © 2019 by Jessica R. Patch

www.Harlequin.com

Printed in U.S.A.

Therefore if any man be in Christ,
he is a new creature: old things are passed away;
behold, all things are become new.
*—2 Corinthians* 5:17

To Dad—for giving me a love for spy movies,
especially James Bond.

## Special Thanks:

My agent, Rachel Kent, who has been one of the biggest
blessings in my life. You are my friend and champion!

My editor, Shana Asaro, who makes everything I write
so much stronger and better. I am thankful for you.

Susan Tuttle, my brainstorming partner and friend.
I wouldn't have a great story if you weren't there
to help me turn it into something worth pursuing.

My family, who always supports, understands
and encourages me to keep writing and dreaming.

# ONE

Grace Thackery was living on a borrowed name; she'd lost every single memory prior to the past year and a half since she'd awakened from a six-month coma. But as she breezed into the kitchen at the Muddy River Inn, inhaling the smell of cinnamon and yeasty dough, she had no doubt she'd loved cinnamon rolls. How could anyone not? She rubbed the round locket around her neck. At least she thought it was a locket, but it wouldn't open—it was as locked as her memories. Had it been a gift from a family member, a friend…a boyfriend, fiancé or husband?

Tish LaMont looked up and grinned, her plump face colored pink from the oven heat; the lines around her lips and eyes showed she'd spent most of her life happy. She slid a pan of rolls onto the butcher block island and waved a pot holder over the steam. "If this rain doesn't let up soon, we'll float away. I can't tell you the last time we had this much in Cottonwood. April showers are supposed to bring May flowers. Not more showers," she drawled in a rich, Mississippi accent.

Grace snickered and helped herself to a cinnamon roll; the fresh hot glaze dripped onto her dessert plate. She'd lick that up last. It had been raining the past eight days straight. Gray and dismal. Something about it felt familiar, teetering on the edge of her fuzzy mind but unwilling to surface. "If I ever lose my memory again, there's no way I'd forget these."

Tish snorted and used her wrist to push away a strand of bobbed gray hair. According to Tish, women over fifty needed to let go and let God. And that meant allowing the silver to rule as a crown of glory and wisdom. Grace wasn't sure what she meant, but it had to be something out of scripture. Tish was the godliest woman Grace had ever met—in the past year and a half, that is.

This woman had taken her under her wing, physically and spiritually, the day Hollister Montgomery—the man who'd rescued her—brought her to Tish. She'd given her a place to live, turning the garden shed into a small living quarter, and in return Grace helped Tish around the inn for a meager, but livable, salary. A man at Hollis's church had given her a car. Once she got behind the wheel, the muscle memory had taken over. Weird thing about retrograde amnesia—she'd lost some words but not her procedural memory. She might not remember the name for a spoon, but she could drive a car or even ride a bike if she'd done it often in her past. Hollis insisted she take lessons and a driver's test anyway. He'd worked with the sheriff to get her a temporary ID and license.

"You going to the facility today?" Tish asked, and pointed to her search-and-rescue raincoat.

"Yep. I told Hollis I'd help him do inventory."

"Hmm," Tish said and gave her a knowing eye. The one she always gave when Grace mentioned him.

Grace couldn't have romantic feelings for Hollis— or anyone. How could she? What if she was already married—or in a relationship and her beloved was out there hunting for her, worried sick? And even if that weren't the case, what did a woman with no memory have to offer? Nothing. Literally. She could see a first date now: Where did you grow up? I don't know. What do you love to do in your spare time? I can't remember. Do you have any brothers or sisters? Maybe.

Tish pointed toward the small dining area for guests. "Not many today. The two businessmen from Memphis. The Westcott couple. And a man from Jackson." She rubbed her hands on her apron. "Before you head out—and take Hollis a couple of those cinnamon rolls—would you carry these into the dining room?"

"You got it." She licked her fingers and washed her hands, then carried a platter of glazed goodness to the buffet in the dining area. She nodded a hello to guests she recognized and spotted the man from Jackson, Mississippi, at the table by the window, sipping coffee and gazing at the rain. He glanced her way as if he felt her watching, but made no move to be polite, to smile or even acknowledge he had locked eyes on her.

"Good morning," she said softly and set the tray of sweets next to the bowl of fresh fruit. "Tish makes homemade cinnamon rolls that are out of this world."

He said nothing, only stared.

"Are you okay, sir?" She moved closer to his table. Was he having a stroke? His fist tightened, and he cocked his head. "Sir?"

He blinked out of his stupor. "Fine. Sorry. I'm fine. I'm Peter Rainey."

"Grace Thackery."

"You work here or just doing a favor?" he asked and studied her. Not in an uncomfortable way, but curious.

"For almost two years now." She granted him a

smile and he returned it, dimples creasing deep into his cheeks.

He rubbed the stubble on his chin, a shade darker than his close-cropped blond hair. "And before that?"

"This and that." Probably. Surely. She shrugged. "So, what are you in town doing?" Her lack of memory was no one's entertainment. It was a horror story at best.

"Business."

Grace checked her watch. "Well, I hope it goes well. If you need an umbrella, Tish keeps extras by the front door." She waved and bustled to the kitchen. Before opening it, she tossed a look at Mr. Rainey. He was still watching her, his eyebrows pulled together creating a line across his brow. He couldn't possibly know her. Could he? If so, why wouldn't he have said something? She shook off the thought and snagged the to-go box of cinnamon rolls for Hollis, then she poured a cup of coffee and snapped the plastic lid over it.

She hollered a quick goodbye as Tish stirred a vat of gravy for biscuits and then she rushed into the steady rain. Once inside the small four-door Honda Civic, she removed her hood and set off for the SAR facility. She'd been volunteering at the search-and-rescue organization for over a year. It had started out to keep her busy while she was acclimating to her new normal, but when she discovered she loved the outdoors, hiking and had several survival skills—including tying a slip knot like a pro—Hollis had suggested she take the classes to join the volunteer team. Maybe she'd been a Girl Scout troop leader.

Being a part of a team and helping others had been a lifesaver for Grace. Guess Hollis suspected she needed to feel useful. He was intuitive and patient. Always going the extra mile to help others, including Grace.

He'd made sure she had a place to live, to work, and he'd also taken her to church on Sundays. She couldn't remember if she'd ever given her heart and life to God, but after a few months of attending she felt the urge to make the commitment.

The women had been kind and helpful, inviting her to Bible studies and quilting classes—she was a natural with a needle and thread—but the love and friendship she'd been lavished with still didn't combat the night-time warring where she wrestled with who she was—who she'd been. Did she want to be that person again? Were her interests and likes now the same as the woman once before? Would she ever know?

As she turned on Old Highway 4, a pop sounded and the car jerked to the right. The smell of rubber stamped out the homey scent of coffee and cinnamon. She veered off the shoulder and parked. Clambering out into the rain, she spotted the right front tire blown, tread hanging limply on the ground. Growling under her breath, she opened the trunk and hauled out the jack and the spare. Hey! She knew how to fix a tire. It was all there in her mind. Score. Maybe she was a mechanic. Or she had an attentive father who wanted her to be independent. Or a husband…boyfriend…brother?

She knelt in the wet puddle and went to work.

Headlights stabbed through the dappled haze. A pickup eased onto the shoulder of the road. She waved as two men clambered out and headed toward her. Both wearing jeans and work boots.

"I got it, fellas, but thanks for getting out in the rain to help a lady." Were the people where she once lived as cordial?

The shorter, stockier man didn't smile and the taller one ran a hand through his black rain-slicked hair—his eyes glinted like a shark's. Grace's neck hairs stood at attention and a pit of dread hollowed out her gut.

"I see you have a little trouble, eh?" The taller man shot her a wild smile, and the hungry animal gleam in his eyes said he very well may have done something to give her this trouble.

"No…no," she stammered. "I'm doing fine on my own." Rain trickled down her face and she gripped the jack as the stockier man edged to the left of her and the one speaking stalked her dead-on.

"We just want to know where the doctor is."

Grace's heart hammered in her chest as she jumped to her feet, her knees like jelly and her hands trembling. It was pretty clear they weren't talking about Dr. Jones, the local General Practitioner. "You…you stay back. I don't know anything about a doctor."

He laughed. "Don't play stupid. All you have to do is tell us the truth and no harm comes to you. But if you hold out…"

She backed up a step and right into the chest of the shorter Latino. He gripped her upper arms with force. "You hold out and we mess you up. Where's the doctor? We won't ask again." He hurled Spanish slurs and she recognized them. She knew Spanish! At least the bad words. His fingers dug into her arms and she winced. Tears burned her eyes. "You don't understand. I really can't help you. I was hurt—"

"Now you're hurt," the jerk gripping her said, and slung her to the ground into a thick puddle of muddy water saturating the grass. His boot landed on the back of her head, forcing her face into the water. Panic raced through her veins and then into her throat, clogging it with a suppressed scream.

This was going to end terribly.

Grace's lungs lit on fire with the need to consume air.

Suddenly her right foot connected with his groin, as if it had a mind of its own, releasing his boot from her head. She flipped on her back, gulped in the air, rose up and grabbed the man hunching over her by his shirt collar, pulling him toward her and the ground while placing her feet on his chest. She rolled back into the soggy earth, using the momentum to flip the man over her body and into the taller guy.

They both crumpled into the spongey grass.

How had she done that? The shorter attacker growled and told the other guy, in Spanish, to get a handle on her. Before she had a good clear thought she launched toward the man making it to his feet and muscled him toward the car, then she shoved his head onto the hood with so much force it reverberated through her entire arm. He collapsed and didn't move.

The last assailant grabbed her hair and she bent forward, tossing him over her, then clutched the jack and slammed it into his head.

Grace dropped it when he went still. Oh no. What had she done? Her body trembled with total fear—from the men, from her behavior. Flight mode kicked in and she sprinted the two miles to the SAR facility.

She busted into Hollis's office, startling him out of his chair. "I'm a ninja!" she squawked, panting for breath, dripping wet. "I'm a...*ninja*!" She frantically shook her head, disbelief washing over her again as the scenario replayed through her brain. "I thought I was a chef or a Girl Scout leader. But I'm a ninja! I'm a ninja—"

She assaulted a man with a jack! Yes, he came at her first...but she didn't even hesitate. A weird predatory urge had taken over and she...she... What had she done?

"Grace," Hollis said in a calming but wary tone as he swung around the desk, his dark-eyed gaze giving her the strength she needed. "I need you to breathe, honey. Slow down. Let's press Pause. Get your bearings." He pushed a mass of wet hair from her face and tipped her chin up so he could look into her eyes. "Focus," he drawled in his rich baritone voice that always brought her comfort.

"You don't understand." He hadn't witnessed her takedown, beating them like ragdolls with no thought whatsoever. "I have kung fu moves. And I know *Spanish*!" She told him in perfect Spanish she was a ninja and she thought she'd killed a man.

Hollis's eyes widened. "What man?"

"Hollis, you know Spanish too?" Of course, he did. He was a former navy SEAL. He'd done a few tours. She was no navy SEAL. But it sure felt like it out there. "I know I'm not making any sense." Her blood froze and she shivered. The room tipped.

"You're going into shock." Hollis raced to the lockers on the far side of the wall and grabbed a blanket, wrapping it around her. He lifted her eyelids. "Pupils are dilated." He cupped her face. "Look at me. Inhale. Exhale." He rubbed her forearms, working to generate body heat, then he enveloped her, working his hands down her back. "Keep breathing."

His voice soothed her, his touch eased her knotted muscles as she followed his instructions. Slowly she gained her wits, until the hysteria passed and she could rationally think. "Hollis, two Latino men pulled up behind me on the highway. My tire blew. I'm pretty sure they set it up." She told him what happened next and how she singlehandedly put them on the ground. Grace had almost been murdered; the fear was overwhelming.

Didn't matter that she had defended herself. She had been *harmed*. Might be attacked again. She collapsed into his powerful arms. "I can't be a murderer, Hollis."

Hollis held her tighter and she melded into him—a safe place. The safest place she'd been since she'd lost her memory, possibly ever. He smelled like oranges and fabric softener. His dark stubble scraped against her cheek as he soothed her with soft *shhs*. She peered into his eyes, almost as dark as hers, searching for wisdom, answers…hope.

"It's going to be okay. Let's go to the site. Figure it out." He lifted the collar of her jacket. "First go get some fatigues and get dry, then meet me here." She frantically nodded and did as he instructed. When she returned, she'd wrung out her hair and wrapped it in a wet knot at the base of her neck. She wore khaki fatigues and her spare pair of hiking boots she kept at the facility.

Hollis scrutinized her. "You ready?"

No. She was terrified. Either someone had mistaken her for someone she wasn't. Or Grace had secrets that were so dark, she didn't ever want to remember.

Hollis kept his emotions close to the vest. He didn't want to cause further panic, didn't want Grace to be even more afraid, and showing his concern would set her off. Calmly, he escorted her to his pickup and opened the door for her. "It's going to be okay," he reassured her again. When he'd found her two years ago during SAR dive drills in the river, she'd been roughed up and left for dead on the bank. She was seizing and frothing at the mouth. He feared the trauma had affected her brain and she'd never recover. By the time he got her to the hospital, she was unresponsive, but breathing, though shallow. Then she'd slipped into a coma.

The Grace he knew today might not be the Grace she used to be.

He rounded the truck and climbed in the cab. Grace wrung her slender hands—hands that had a few scars—and chewed on lips that should be kissed not tortured with worrisome gnawing. She was beautiful. Lightly bronzed skin—like the sun had kissed her—and hair as thick and black as night matching her eyes, and long lashes that reminded him of a Southern belle fan. She'd been extremely toned and sculpted when he'd found her, which told him she was a health nut, and the dress she'd been wearing exposed most of her back, revealing scars there as well.

His friend and ER nurse, Daphne, had overstepped HIPAA and confirmed that Grace had past injuries. Broken bones. Two arms. A collarbone. Her right leg. Left ankle. Several fingers. Hollis immediately suspected domestic abuse, but no one came calling for her. He'd called in a favor with an old SEAL buddy who ran a private security company now, but his search hadn't turned up anything. He had done a missing persons check to see if anyone of her description had vanished around the time Hollis had found Grace, but no one matching her physical appearance had. And without knowing her name, her birthdate or any information that would aid in a background check or missing person's report, it made things practically impossible. With her scars and broken bones, Hollis and the sheriff had agreed it was best to search for her identity discreetly. If the person who had injured Grace resurfaced, and she didn't know him or her—and neither did Hollis nor Sheriff Freeman—then Grace was a sitting duck. What quiet investigating and inquiry they had done all hit dead ends. It was as if Grace didn't exist.

Except she did and it was mind-boggling. Nothing but grace she survived. Day in and out Hollis came and sat at her bedside, talking with her even though she was unresponsive. He needed to call her something. Grace fit. Thackery was his great grandmother's name. It wasn't like he could call her Grace Montgomery. Then one day he was reading her a psalm and her eyelids flickered…once…twice and those coffee bean–colored eyes looked into his. For a split second it was like she knew him. Had heard every word he'd ever spoken or read to her. He thought she might even say his name, but then it registered she had no idea where she was or even who she was. Couldn't recall a single thing and hysteria had set in.

He quietly drove through the rain, waiting for her to speak now.

Finally, she did. She told him in further detail what had happened. "Do you think I learned self-defense?"

That was the rational woman he'd come to know and admire. He smirked. "Already tossed the ninja theory out? I kinda liked it."

Grace playfully frowned at his teasing. "I'm not quiet enough to be a ninja."

"I'll attest. You barreled into my office and scared my socks off." He glanced in the rearview mirror. Just in case. "It's possible you learned self-defense or martial arts." Health nut *and* martial arts or kickboxing—both great exercises. Or she may have taken it up to protect herself from whoever inflicted those wounds and had broken her body. One theory was her husband or boy-friend discovered she was leaving and tracked her, gave her the beating of her life and left her for dead. But she was wearing a red dress and heels. Someone running away wouldn't have been in that flimsy—and slightly provocative—dress. There were other theories, but they were darker and Hollis didn't let his mind wander there.

"What if I did kill them? What will happen?" she asked softly.

"It was self-defense." They approached Grace's car—no other vehicle around.

"The truck is gone!" Grace threw off her seat belt and bolted from the vehicle before it got good and stopped, darting toward her car, ignoring the drizzle. "No one is here!" Her voice held a measure of fear and relief. She hadn't killed anyone. Good. But they were gone and that meant they could return. Not good. Hollis stood beside her and squatted, inspecting the tire.

"It's been punctured by a blade of some kind. They must have stabbed it before you left the inn this morning, then followed you waiting on it to blow."

"I don't understand, Hollis. This makes no sense."

But it might if she had her memories. "If you gave them a solid whupping like you say you did—if that was a skill they were aware of—then they aren't going to believe you have no memory."

"It's retrograde amnesia!" she protested and Hollis snorted. "What? What is so amusing?"

"I doubt two probable criminals care or know much about amnesia. All they know is you kicked their butts from here to Timbuktu, and they've gone to lick their injured pride."

Grace's cheeks paled. "And when it's been mended?"

"They'll return with new tactics." Likely the kind that don't involve getting too close. That triggered a new wave of panic through his chest, squeezing it tight.

"Like the kind they can administer from a distance?"

Too perceptive. He kinda dug it. "I wasn't going to say that but…yeah." He changed her tire and wiped his wet, dirty hands on his jeans. "It'll be okay, though, Grace. I'm not going to let anyone hurt you."

"Gonna be on me like blue on sky."

He chuckled and opened her driver's-side door for her. "Something like that."

"You know," she said wistfully, "I'm handy with a needle and thread, and that time Dennis fell into the ravine I knew how to splint his arm. If these guys are looking for a doctor... I could be a doctor or in the medical field too."

"Anything is possible. I'll follow you to the inn. Drive slow on the spare. I'll have it fixed later today."

She nodded and cranked her engine. A doctor? Hmm...doubtful, but for now he'd keep his thoughts to himself. He wasn't sure he liked where they were going.

Inside the inn, Grace snagged a leftover cinnamon roll. She deserved it. She also deserved to get clean. Her face was a mess, muddy and streaked from the battle a little over an hour ago.

"Hollis, I'm going to take care of all this filth. When I'm done, we can get back to the facility. I need to look at the weather satellites, and I know you want to ride out and inspect the waters around the levee."

Hollis finished off his roll and nodded. "You really should. You smell."

"I do not!"

Laughing, he held his mug up in a salute and winked. "Maybe not, but you do look like you wallowed in mud."

She shuddered. She had and not by choice.

"I didn't mean to upset you." His eyes held concern.

"You didn't. I need to clear the gunk off my face." She headed for the kitchen door.

"Holler if you need anything."

Her place from the kitchen was about fifteen to twenty feet. Grace waved and made her way out the door and along the sidewalk lined with flower pots— the flowers wilting at the merciless and unending rain. It was overcast but warm. After unlocking her door, she stepped inside and tensed.

Something wasn't right. Pausing in the entry, she grabbed an umbrella from the wicker basket. Nothing appeared out of sorts. But the eerie sensation skittered across her skin. Everything inside her screamed a warning. Should she call for Hollis? The window in the inn's kitchen was open. He'd hear. Grace surveyed the open floor plan. To the left of the kitchenette was her bedroom and bathroom. Inching toward her room, her heart galloped. Was she being ridiculous?

She toed her bedroom door farther open and stepped inside, caught a whiff of musk. The smell zinged along her memory pulling something familiar forward, but it was blurry. She inched into the bathroom, switched on the light and felt a presence behind her.

Turning, a figure loomed. Throat constricting, adrenaline racing, she didn't wait for him to tackle her. She went on the offensive and rushed him, but he dodged her. She swung around and his back was to her. Grace instinctively thrust out the umbrella—the hook catching around his neck like a noose. She yanked—choking him—forcing him backward and toward her.

"You…always…knew how…to make…an entrance…" he sputtered and held his arms out to his side. "I'm not here to hurt you."

"Then what are you here for? My valuables? I'll give you a hint. I don't have any." Where on earth did that bravado and snark come from or her instincts to use that umbrella as a weapon?

"I'm turning around."

She recognized his voice now that her ears weren't buzzing, but her heart was going wild and she itched to run. Run fast and hard.

With hands raised, Peter Rainey from breakfast faced her. "You can put the umbrella down. Really."

She lowered it.

"I thought you were dead." He shook his head, eyes wide. "But then three weeks ago I saw you on the national news. In the background while the SAR chief told the world they'd found the little girl their team had been searching for. It was covered almost nightly. I was in shock. Then confused."

He was confused? How had he seen her on TV? Hollis had made sure to steer her clear from the media during that hunt for their pastor's little girl—her scars kept him protective of her, and she appreciated that. She hadn't found the child for the recognition anyway.

"Why did you settle down in this Podunk town? Why did you pretend not to know me earlier? And why are you volunteering with Search and Rescue and living under a tin roof?"

"Why are you under my tin roof? I don't have any cinnamon rolls here." Now probably wasn't the time to go comedic and dry, but a memory teetered on the edge of her mind—she used this kind of banter to do something...what?

He chuckled. "Always loved that snark. I know you hate me."

She did?

"I'm here to make amends, Max, even though you have every right to stomp me into the ground for betraying you. I should have known better but..."

Max! Was that her name? Short for Maxine or something? She glanced at the door and her hands shook.

Peter spotted it. "Are...are you afraid?"

She was working hard to conceal it; should she not be? "Well, you did betray me." If she told him her brain had deflated like a balloon and she was at a loss for memory, he might try to hurt her or clam up. He'd asked why she pretended not to know him. Well, he hadn't acted like he knew her either, so he was hiding something. He was her only link to her past. She had to play the game for as long as she could.

"Look, I'll tell you everything, but I may not be the only one who knows you're alive."

Oh so true. She had two creeps coming for her already.

Peter sighed. "I can help you. I know you have no reason to trust me, but I promise I'm telling you the truth. Where is Dr. Sayer? I can help her too."

Her! The doctor had a name and gender. Good, she could work with this. But could she work with this man? What if he tried to betray her again? How did he betray her before? By beating her up and leaving her for dead? Her hands wouldn't stop shaking, and she bit down on her lip to hide the tremble. What if she didn't know any more self-defense moves?

"I didn't—" He paused, cocked his head and surveyed her. It gave her the shivers but she tried to hold fast. Still, her fingers jittered, causing the umbrella to bounce. He watched it then let his gaze slowly roll over her face and locked onto her eyes again.

"What's my name?" He was on to her somehow. The fear. The fear was tipping him off that something was wrong.

"Peter."

He narrowed his eyes and took a step forward. She took a step back and he paused, tipped his head to the side. "What's *your* name?"

Busted. Would he kill her now?

"Why do you ask?" She tossed a glance at the open door and took another step toward it.

Peter matched a step forward for every one she took in retreat, surprise in his eyes. "I thought you were toying with me this morning somehow so I didn't say anything, played the game. But you weren't up to anything sneaky. You don't know me. And you don't know *you* either. I'm so sorry, Max."

"For what?"

"Everything. It was all lies."

"What was all lies? Is my name Max?" she asked, her head spinning. Did she try to run or did she trust this man who admitted to betraying her?

He glanced out the window and shook his head; he seemed concerned. "No. It's a nickname. Mad Max."

Mad Max? "Am I crazy or something? If you're not here to hurt me…then tell me who I am."

"Max," he whispered. "Your real name is—"

Glass shattered and Peter fell to the ground dead. Grace stared at him frozen and stunned, then another bullet slammed into the wall by her head. "Hollis!" she screamed and hit the floor.

# TWO

Hollis hit the door running when the first shot cracked through the air and was at Grace's front door as she screamed for him. "I'm here," he called and slid across the floor to her. "Stay low." He glanced into her bedroom and did a double take. A body lay on the floor. "Who is that?"

"Peter Rainey," she breathed, her face deathly pale.

"You remember?" Had memories surfaced in the last ten minutes? Questions would have to wait. He needed to get Grace to safety. Hopefully, the shooter wouldn't open fire on people in a public place. It was his only chance. Once she was out of danger, he would inspect the woods, then find out who the dead guy was in her bedroom. They huddled on the floor for several moments. The gunfire had ceased. The shooter could be changing positions, windows. Getting a better line of fire. Was it one of those men from earlier or someone new?

The woods covered the south of her house. North was the inn. No decent place there to find accurate cover or to get a good shot. "We're going out the front door and making a dash to the inn. You ready?"

"Not really," she groused. "But let's go."

"One, two, three!" He hauled her up but kept her hunched as he shielded her with his body. They sprinted across the wet walkway to the inn. Inside he slammed the door and kicked a kitchen chair into the corner. No windows. No easy target. He lowered her into the chair. Grace's face retained the muddy streaks from earlier and strands of dark hair had come loose from its bun, sticking to her neck.

"I want you to stay here. I'll be right back." Hollis gripped Grace's shoulders. "Promise me."

She nodded as Tish entered the kitchen. "What in the world is going on? I heard the door slam and a ruckus in here…"

"Grace is in danger, Tish." He gave her the short version, and with every word her face blanched even further until she looked like a walking snowdrift. "I believe she'll be okay since the inn is full of people—though I can't be one hundred percent sure, but still…keep an eye out." He looked at Grace. "Call the sheriff. Chances are no one paid attention to the shots." Gunfire wasn't unfamiliar in the South, in this town—even Tish hadn't been drawn into the kitchen from the gunfire, but from their commotion. "I'll be back." Hollis wanted his own time to search and he'd have it if he moved fast. Probably the SEAL in him, but he wanted dibs on any clues that might give them more information on the deceased and Grace's identity.

Grace nodded.

"We'll be fine." Tish headed for the cherry-red tea kettle on the stove.

Tish had mettle and Hollis loved her for it. He retrieved his ankle weapon and slipped outside into the woods. After about five minutes, he found one man's footprints in the mud. Fairly large. Hollis aimed his

Glock toward the garden house. Perfect angle. Clean shot. Good distance away. No casings. Looked like the shooter had collected the brass, meaning he might be and probably was a professional.

He followed the prints about a mile until they tracked to an old back road. The shooter either cased the place for a few days, finding the best way to enter and escape undetected, or he was familiar with the area—a local or someone who frequented Cottonwood. The inn was rife with businessmen and women who'd rather stay in a cozy home for a week than an impersonal hotel. But why would a local want to hurt Grace or kill Peter Rainey? And who?

He hurried to Grace's, wiping his muddy boots on her mat, then he entered. Under her sink he found a pair of yellow cleaning gloves and slid his hands into them, then he strode into the bedroom. He studied the scene. The last thing Hollis wanted to do was move the body, but he needed to inspect the wound. The air smelled like iron and Grace's vanilla candles. Appeared to be a rifle shot. A possible sniper.

He carefully rummaged through pockets, searching for identification, credit cards, anything. The only thing on the man was a wallet with two hundred bucks and a single peppermint in his right jean pocket. Who traveled with no identification?

Someone who didn't want to reveal their identity.

What had Grace been immersed in? He'd suspected an abusive relationship, and that was still a possibility, though it seemed much slimmer with the earlier attack and now this.

Hollis used his cell phone camera and snapped a picture of the guy, then swept the perimeter. No sign of danger. Back inside, Grace's face and hands were clean and she'd redone the bun; this time it was higher on her head. Tish sat beside her with a cup of tea as they murmured to one another.

"I just hung up with Sheriff Freeman." Grace stood, hope and dread vied for first place in her gaze. "What did you find?"

Hollis hated being the bearer of bad news. "Nothing. Let's go through his room before Sheriff Freeman arrives. We don't have much time." Once Cord Freeman showed up, which could be any minute, Hollis feared he'd be out of the loop. Even if they worked closely on occasional rescue missions, Cord was a stickler for rules. Hollis might have to bend some in order to protect Grace and he didn't want anyone—not even Cord—standing in the way. He turned to Tish. "Can we have a pair of those latex gloves you clean with?"

Tish made haste and gave him a pair, worry in her eyes. Hollis laid a hand on her shoulder. "It's going to be okay." He kept saying that, but the truth was he had no idea if it was or not. "Come on." He gave the gloves to Grace. She followed him through the dining area, into the foyer and to the front entrance where the stairs were located. They climbed up and around to the second floor. Found Peter Rainey's room and entered. Tish said he'd arrived late last night.

"Did you find a driver's license?" Grace asked as she opened and closed drawers. Hollis spotted a rolling suitcase in the corner of the room. Carry-on size.

"No. He had a wallet but only cash inside. Odd, don't you think?" He carefully unzipped the black Samsonite carry-on bag. A pair of jeans. Button-down shirt. Socks…toiletry bag.

"It is odd." Grace finished with the dresser and headed for the chest of drawers. "He told me that he calls me 'Mad Max' as a nickname. What does that mean?"

Hollis paused perusing the suitcase and glanced at Grace. Mad Max was a cop who'd lost his son and sought revenge. He was a wild card, but excellent at his job. "It's from a movie. A series of movies. Mad Max was a good guy." He left it at that and filed away what the nickname might mean in context to Grace. "What else did he say?"

"Our doctor is female and her name is Dr. Sayer. He didn't know I had amnesia until he noticed I was scared. That signaled something was wrong. I guess I shouldn't have been afraid of him. He also said he was sorry for betraying me."

Hollis's stomach knotted. Could they have been romantically involved? Had he betrayed her with infidelity? "Tell me everything."

As they combed the room, finding nothing, she laid out the details. This guy carried light and had zero identification. How did he fly? Or drive? "We need to find his car." Peter's keys had been on the nightstand.

Outside, they spotted Cord's sheriff's unit. He'd bypassed finding them for the crime scene. Typical. "We need to hurry."

Grace nodded and they rushed to the white sedan Peter had been driving. Nothing of value or telling inside. Just maps of Mississippi and stacks of brochures in the glove box for surrounding towns. Doubtful he was a sightseer. No, when he'd seen Grace was alive, he'd come straight for her.

When little Lilly's disappearance in the state park had gone national, Hollis feared whoever hurt Grace would see her and come to finish what they started. It's why he'd flown home early from his sister Greer's house in Alabama. Now that Greer and Locke were together and engaged… "Remember me telling you about my sister's fiancé?"

"The one who chases tornadoes for a living? What about him?" Grace asked.

"His sister is former Secret Service and now works with their cousin and a specialized team at a private security company in Atlanta. I also know the head of the company—he's a former SEAL too. He looked into your case when you were in a coma, but obviously nothing turned up." With these new developments, it was time to try again. "But they have skills that can get us information far faster than the local sheriff's department. How about I call them again. Maybe we can dig up some information on Dr. Sayer, Peter Rainey and those Latino men."

Grace gnawed the tip of her thumb. "I'm up for anything that gets me answers. He said others might know I'm alive. Why does that feel ominous?"

The sheriff rounded the corner on foot. Cord Freeman was a hulk of a man and as rough as a corn cob. A few years older than Hollis's thirty-two years and serious about everything. He nodded at Grace, lingering a bit longer than necessary—like most men in town. She was striking and exotic. "Grace, Hollister."

"Hey, Cord," Hollis said.

Cord eyed his gloves, then Grace's. "I see you've been playing CSI. I'm going to assume you weren't dumb enough to disturb the evidence."

Hollis's jaw twitched but he reined in his temper. Cord had a point. "I'm not a complete idiot."

Cord raised a dark eyebrow. Amusement gleamed in his eyes. He was mad, but not livid. "Well…at least you admit you're half an idiot." He smirked. "What'd you find?" Cord asked a million questions and scratched his head. The coroner arrived and Cord followed him to Grace's. Hollis held Grace back with him. "I know things feel like they're crazier than ever, but let's look at it like the glass is half full. We now have a few pieces of information. Names. We can make this dog hunt."

She reached up and lightly touched his cheek, no longer wearing the gloves. He hadn't shaved this morning, but his stubble didn't seem to bother her. "Hollis, I don't know what I would have done—what I would do—without you. I will never be able to repay you."

He caressed the hand resting on his cheek, his heart swelling and aching in unison. "I don't want to be repaid, Grace. I just want you to know who you are." And who she might belong to. He wanted her unlocked from this prison of her mind. Free to... He wouldn't go there. "I'm going to call Locke and have him see if his sister can help us. If I can't reach him, I'll call Wilder directly."

More deputies showed up and filed into Grace's house. Her brow turned worried. "I hope this doesn't mess up business for Tish. She's worked hard to build this inn after Ed died, and having a shooting on the property isn't exactly the picture of cozy and safe. What if they see the cadaver?"

*Cadaver.* A word that flowed off her tongue like it belonged there. She might be in the medical field... but he held reservations. A man with no identification found Grace...and wanted the doctor. Said he could be trusted. Two obvious bad guys wanted said doctor as well. Why would Grace know about this person's whereabouts? Could Dr. Sayer be in the Witness Protection Program? He liked the idea of Grace being a marshal a whole lot more than a woman with a seedy past—possibly criminal. Hollis couldn't imagine Grace would desire to return to that environment if her memories surfaced. He was there the Sunday she walked to the front and gave her heart and life to God. She was a new person now. But the needling inside him intensified. Reminded him of his own past.

Mary Beth had been a bright and shining star when he'd moved to Cottonwood to take over the SAR several years ago. He'd fallen fast and thought she returned those feelings, but after a year she claimed she didn't know who she was and needed to find herself. Whatever that meant. She'd asked for three months, and Hollis had agreed with hopes she'd return from New York ready to move forward in their relationship.

But instead, she'd decided small-town life wasn't for her. It was mundane. Too small. Not enough excitement. She ought to be here now. Mary Beth would have more excitement than she could handle.

She'd broken Hollis's heart, and all but told him *he* wasn't enough. He'd managed to get over the fact that his dad had walked out on his family, but Mary Beth stomping on his heart seemed different. Didn't matter now. It was water under the bridge. Which reminded him. "I'd like to take a boat out and check river levels." He peered into the sky. "I don't see this letting up." They had levees in place, but if this didn't level off soon, he wasn't sure what would happen. Being a water town had its perks, but also its fears.

"The rain or what's happening to me?" Grace muttered.

Truthfully?

Both.

Grace watched as they discreetly carried the body of Peter Rainey from her home. She answered additional questions for Sheriff Freeman, though she had only so much to offer. After that hoopla wore off and a crew had come in and cleaned for her, she and Hollis sat on her worn gray couch and he made a call to Locke and then to Jody Novak, Locke's sister. They put her and the team at Covenant Crisis Management on Speaker and Hollis relayed everything that had happened.

Wheezer, their computer analyst, had jumped on the search and according to the team, if there was something to be found he would find it. Grace hoped so. Once again, she prayed and asked God to reveal her past so she could move forward.

"Okay," Wheezer said over the speaker, "I have a pretty large list of Dr. Sayers. Cutting down to female. Less of a list. I'm going to filter the search to doctors who went off-grid in the past two years. It'll take a minute, but when I have something, I'll call you."

"Hang in there," Wilder Flynn, the security team director, said to Grace. "We won't stop until we have answers. If you need us there, Hollister, say the word. I can send a team member or personally fly in."

"I appreciate that, Wilder. For right now, I think we can manage."

Grace did, too, but flying blind was dangerous. Anyone could be against her. She wouldn't recognize an enemy from an ally. They hung up and she offered to make coffee.

Hollis grinned. "I never turn down coffee."

Grace actually laughed. As she headed for the coffee pot in her kitchenette, she glanced inside her bedroom and a sudden wave came over her. A memory! Like a scene from a movie playing in full color in her mind.

Grace was dressed in a long black evening gown, her hair swept to the side. She had her arm looped into a man's and as she gazed up, it was Peter Rainey's face. He laid his hand on hers, and that's when she noticed the engagement ring. Peter leaned down and kissed her. "You look beautiful, Max," he said.

Then the memory was gone. Fade to black.

She fumbled the carafe and it slipped from her hands, crashing to the floor. Hollis jumped up from the couch. "Grace?"

"Sorry... I uh—I dropped the coffee pot. Don't come over here. Glass." She rushed to the small pantry and retrieved a broom, but her hands shook. What did this mean? Had she been engaged—married even—to Peter? His betrayal could have been adultery. She'd had little moments of memory pops over the past six months but nothing this big. This substantial. This confusing. Grace went to task sweeping up the glass shards.

"What startled you?" Hollis asked.

Heat ballooned in her cheeks. She couldn't hide this from Hollis. But everything in her wanted to keep it buried. "I... I had a flash of a memory. A snippet really, and it unnerved me. Came on so sudden."

Hollis ignored her warning about the glass and leaned over the breakfast bar, resting his elbows on it and putting himself eye level with her. "What was it?"

"I'm not sure what it meant," she whispered as she dared a peek at him. Solemn eyes. Jaw tight. As if bracing himself for the worst news. What would be the worst news to Hollis? Had she once loved Peter? He'd never mentioned any feelings. Granted, he hadn't had much time before he was murdered. It was as if someone knew he would talk, and they were shutting him up.

Instead of revealing the secret, she changed the subject. "Someone wanted Peter dead. He was going to tell me who I was and possibly answer any further questions I may have had."

Hollis's lips twisted to the side as he pondered the information. "If the shooter didn't know you had amnesia, then killing Peter first might not be about him giving you information as much as *you* giving Peter information…as in the doctor's location. If those Latino men wanted the doctor, they could have killed Peter to cut him out of finding her first."

"Excellent point. The guy with the gun may have believed I'd go with Peter. The men who attacked me didn't realize I had amnesia—neither did Peter at first. If they're behind killing Peter, your theory makes more sense."

Hollis nodded. "I wonder if he was truly your ally. He said to trust him, but he also said he'd betrayed you."

"He mentioned it had all been lies. What does *all* mean?"

Hollis's phone rang, and he answered. "…Okay. Location? We're on our way. I got Grace with me." He hung up. "Two teenage boys out fishing on the river. With the rain and flow, they can't paddle in. Need a tow."

Grace left the broom and a pile of glass on the kitchen floor and followed Hollis outside to his truck. "Why would teenage boys be in the fast-flowing Mississippi River, knowing all the water—"

"One, they are teenage boys. Two, teenage boys have no sense. I know. I was one. And I'm sure there was a dare involved. They're going to be grounded for a century." Hollis chuckled but it didn't quite hit the jovial mark. They could drown out there.

They stopped at the SAR facility. Hollis hitched the trailer to his truck and loaded the boat onto the trailer while Grace grabbed extra life vests. They headed west on Old Highway 4 until they reached the parking lot at the river's boat ramp entrance. Grace backed the boat down the ramp and they lowered it into the water, put their life vests on and sped across the choppy waters toward the location the boys had given the 911 dispatcher.

Grace pointed ahead. They were bobbing in a little johnboat. "You're right. They have no sense at all."

Hollis pulled the boat close and tossed a rope. Then he leaped into the boys' johnboat, rocking it wildly. Both boys sat quietly. No doubt dreading the parental punishment to come. Once he tied the rope, he said something to the boys and they nodded. "We need life vests, Grace. They seem to have *lost* theirs."

Both boys hung their heads as Grace tossed two over.

"I'm going to ride with them. Pull us in," Hollis said.

Grace nodded and slid into the captain's seat, revved the engine and carefully turned the boat, so she didn't tip the little one behind her. She towed them to the ramp. The older teen hopped out and ran and got his truck, then backed the trailer into the water as the other boy and Hollis secured their boat on the trailer.

"Don't run off just yet," Hollis called. "Park up there and wait on me."

After securing their own boat, they pulled up beside the boys, hopped out and reclaimed the vests.

"They are sorely regretting this decision," Hollis whispered, amusement lining his words. He gave them a stern warning about boating in the river—especially when it was this high and without life vests—and said that their parents would be receiving a phone call from him. The boys nodded and gave yes sirs, then Hollis and Grace strolled toward Hollis's truck.

"Well, that was fun," Grace deadpanned and turned

toward the Big Muddy, Hollis leaning on the side of the truck. "River is really high, Hollis. That concerns me."

"Me too."

The boys peeled through the gravel lot, fishtailing and whooping and hollering. Hollis shook his head. "And they learned nothing. They're just going to take their recklessness to the roads."

Grace frowned. "Recklessness. I can't make that definition come." Stuff like this happened all the time, and it was frustrating to no end.

"It means behavior with no thought that it could endanger themselves or others. Or both." He sighed. "Make sense?"

Hollis had been her saving grace these past two years, but now that her life was in danger, was she being reckless by letting him stay involved? He watched her carefully, waiting for her answer. "Yeah," she said quietly. "Makes sense."

"Grace, are you okay? Since the memory flash you've been kinda off. You know you can share anything with me, right? I'm here for you. We're...we're friends." That last sentence seemed hard for him to say. They were friends, though. She couldn't remember ever having any but surely friends cared enough to look out for one another. Hollis was protecting her, but who was protecting him? Not Grace. But down deep came an intense desire...so incredible—to protect him. To guard him. She wasn't even sure she had the ability, but the emotion was so wildly strong that surely she must have the power to back it up.

"I need you to know, Hollis—"

*Pop!*

A bullet whizzed past and Grace winced as a sudden sting seared her skin. Her jacket ripped open near the shoulder. She'd been shot.

Hollis threw her to the ground. "Get under the truck," he hollered and they slid their way underneath. "How bad are you hit?"

"A graze. I think." If it was the same shooter from earlier this morning, he had excellent aim. Either he missed this time or was sending a deadly warning that if she didn't cough up the doctor, next time he wouldn't miss. She squeezed her eyes shut. "I don't know how to make these people understand that the information they want is sealed up tight in my brain!"

"We'll worry about that later. Right now, shimmy out the other side. Stay down, but get inside the cab. I'll wait until you're in before heading for the driver's side."

"No! Hollis, they may shoot you on sight. They have no reason to keep you alive, and they may believe that killing you might make me talk." It wouldn't. The very thought of them hurting Hollis sent a rage she didn't remember ever feeling through her system. It was cold. Dark. And frightening—because for a split second it crossed her mind to make them pay if they hurt him. Deep in her marrow, a whisper said she could do exactly that.

"Don't worry about me, Grace. I'm a big boy and this ain't my first rodeo."

"I know, but—"

"Get in the truck. We can argue later." His voice had the same scolding tone he'd laid on the boys, but she caught a measure of fear behind it—not for him but for her. She scooted until she was free from under the truck, then rolled over and carefully ducked while opening the door.

A bullet slammed into the hitch. Were the shooters

toying with them? "Hollis, you need to come out this side and slide in. I'll drive."

Hollis paused then followed suit. Grace stayed low but scooted over.

Another shot fired. Her arm burned like crazy, and blood had seeped through her shirt and jacket.

Hollis jumped in, and Grace hit the gas, the truck throwing up gravel and fishtailing through the parking lot. She kept the pedal to the metal until they neared the SAR facility. Hollis had remained quiet, his jaw clenched. Once they jumped out, he rounded on her with fire in his eyes. "Grace! I can't believe you!"

Grace stepped back stunned. "Me? You're angry with me?"

"You don't change orders in the middle of a mission. It gets your team killed." His voice had risen an octave or two.

"Yet I'm the only one wounded." She shoved her shoulder around so he'd get a good look. Why was she so angry? "I was trying to save your sorry tail from getting your head blown off. That was a Barrett M82A1, thank you very much! And you're mad because you could have—"

"What did you say?" he asked, eyes wide. The anger dissipated.

"I said, I saved your sorry tail?" What had she said? She was fired up and for no good reason—Hollis was right. She hadn't experienced this kind of fury before, and it terrified her that it could be buried deep within her.

"No. You said I could have had my head blown off by a Barrett M82A1. That's a sniper rifle, Grace. A very specific rifle. How do you know that?"

Grace gasped. She had said that. How did she know?

"I recognized the sound. It makes a high-pitched pop." Was she an arms dealer or something? She nearly fainted.

"Grace, could you have been in the military?"

It was a nicer thought than where she was going. "Maybe? Are there female snipers in the military?"

Hollis stared blankly, then blinked. "Only a handful, but yes."

Grace Thackery. Quilter, bed sheet changer, dining server and possibly a US military sniper. "Now what?" she whispered, unsure she wanted her memories back. If she'd been a sniper, maybe she'd been on a mission to rescue the doctor. In Mississippi?

Hollis touched her shoulder. "First we mend this graze. And then, Grace Thackery, Mad Max…we put a rifle in your hands and see if your brain remembers if it loves the feel of it in your hands or not."

# THREE

"Well, Grace…ready or not," Hollis said and pointed to the disassembled rifle lying in its box on the outdoor table. "Let's see if you've done this before."

She hoped she hadn't. Not once. Not ever.

Last night it had rained too much for them to attempt any shooting practice and she simply couldn't bring herself to try and assemble the rifle. But it was Tuesday midmorning and the rain had let up—the heavy clouds were a warning it would make its return, and she had no more excuses. Only a couple of guests had been around to witness the scene yesterday, and Tish handled it with grace and a free night's stay. Plus maple pecan muffins. That alone was worth staying at the Muddy River Inn.

Hollis had insisted on he and Grace staying in adjoining rooms at the inn to be on the safer side. It was clear that no matter what she said to try and push him from this situation and the danger, he wasn't going to back down. A sliver of her felt guilty, but mostly, she felt grateful and protected.

Grace stared at the rifle and her fingers twitched. She didn't remember holding one. Right now, nothing came to mind. She reached out, hesitated. "I feel stupid."

"I say that at least once a week. Maybe today's *your* day of the week."

"I don't know how to do this, Hollis. I'm blank." Except the innate feeling to pick it up and give it a go.

"Touch it. See what happens."

She nodded and licked her lips. The best-case scenario, she couldn't remember because this wasn't something she'd done before—or often enough—for muscle memory to take over. Worst-case? She did know which meant…she'd killed people before. "I don't want to."

"Even if it might give us a lead? Give us more insight to who you might be? And why three men—so far—have come hunting you? The sniper might be one of—or with—the two men who jumped you when your tire blew. But it could have been someone entirely new sent to take out Peter, and now you…or to warn you. I don't know. But that's too many men who want to hurt you, and they have the advantage. I hate that one man wants you dead. So…maybe just…do it for me."

There wasn't anything Grace wouldn't do for Hollister Montgomery.

She nodded and touched the long black case. She picked it up and placed it on the ground. Not the table.

Grace skimmed her fingers across a long piece with…pods. Lower receiver. She extended the bipod on the lower receiver and laid it on the ground. Oh boy.

She grasped the charging handle and pulled against the tension, withdrawing the midlock pin from its holder. A shaky breath let loose and she glanced at Hollis, but he stood with a grim expression, arms folded. He nodded for her to continue.

She slowly allowed the bolt carrier to come forward until there was no longer any spring tension and it rested in the lower receiver. Carefully, she picked up the upper receiver, making sure the barrel extension and feed ramp were correctly aligned.

She closed her eyes and a flash of memory came. She was dressed all in black, carrying the long black case up a flight of stairs.

She opened her eyes and slid the barrel forward until it was fully seated against the barrel stop. Quickly she slid the impact bumper into position, locked the rear pin into the barrel key, followed two more steps and put the upper receiver into position. After a few more swift maneuvers, she placed the midlock pin through the midlock hole in front of the magazine well on the bottom of the rifle until it was fully seated, locking the upper and lower receivers together. Once the receivers were mated, she loaded and inserted the magazine.

She heard the click and tugged on the magazine to ensure it was properly placed.

"Do you want me to shoot it too?" she asked, adjusting the pad to her shoulder and setting her sights.

"Do you want to shoot it?" Hollis asked.

Her stomach leaped and twisted. Fear and excitement rushed her. "I kinda do. See that tree about two hundred yards? There's a broken branch."

"You wanna hit a broken branch." His tone all but screamed "too easy."

"I want to hit that leaf dangling off the end."

Hollis didn't laugh, and she was only sort of joking. "Okay," he whispered.

She set her sights. Looked up, peered through her scope. Grabbed her locket and kissed it, as if she'd done it a hundred times before. She thought she heard Hollis make a noise like a grunt, but she didn't focus on him. She focused on her breathing and the target. Aimed. Fired.

The leaf blew to bits.

A wave of adrenaline raced through her, warming her blood and giving her a serious energy boost. She stood and shook her head. "I was half kidding. I didn't think I could do it."

"I knew you'd do it." He held up a stopwatch. "I knew it when you beat my time. I can assemble this in twenty-four seconds. You did it in twenty-three, and that was with a slow start."

She stared at the rifle, at the stopwatch, at the obliterated leaf. "Who am I?"

"That's what I'd like to know."

How could she remember assembling the gun and even the proper parts by name, but no memory of using it? How had she learned to do this and at such a fast rate? She must have been important in the military. "Wouldn't the military be looking for me if I was still active?"

"They would."

"Don't you think they would have found me?" Her heart missed a beat as terror washed over the high she'd been on. "Why haven't they? Unless…"

"You might not be military, Grace."

She might be something sinister.

Hollis's cell phone rang and he pulled it from his black fatigue pants. "It's CCM." He answered and put it on Speaker. "Hollis and Grace here."

"Hey, guys. It's Wilder."

"And Wheezer," the computer analyst piped in.

"And Wheezer," Wilder said with a chuckle. "Since he's itching to have a chat with y'all, I'll let him give you the news."

Finally, some news after ages of not having any.

"Wheezer here, again."

Grace grinned at Hollis and he returned it.

"Here's what we believe. The Dr. Sayer you're searching for may be Patsy Mae Sayer. Sixty-one years old. Never been married. Works for the CDC but she disappeared two years ago when she worked overseas in Bogota, Colombia. She was researching yellow fever and malaria among refugees, and who knows what other top secret stuff."

Hollis frowned. "Where was she before Bogota? Isn't Atlanta where the CDC is based?"

"She's spent decades in South America—mostly Bogota, but before that, yes. She's from Illinois. Went to school at Yale. She's a genius. PhD, Genetic bioengineer. It's crazy how smart this woman is," Wheezer said.

"I believe this is your doctor," Wilder said. "For one, the timeline fits and no other Dr. Sayer is missing. Bogota may be the key link. If she was there and Latino men have come looking for her, then Colombians make sense. You may be connected to Bogota, Grace."

Grace shivered. Why would she have been there? She couldn't even remember where Colombia was, but she sure as the grass was green could assemble a sniper rifle. "Do you have the skills, Wheezer, to find out how many female snipers are in the military?"

Wheezer chuckled. "I am flattered that you would think that…and I don't know…"

"Some things are off-limits, Wheezer," Wilder said with a cautionary tone. "I don't need the military getting a red flag they've been breached and descending on us."

Right. True. Grace was desperate.

"And even if I could—which I might—it would take a long time to crack through the number of firewalls and encrypted security. Do you think you might be a sniper in the military?" he asked.

No. She was afraid she was a gun for hire or something equally as terrifying. But the Colombian men didn't think the doctor was dead. Which meant Grace hadn't been sent to kill her. Kidnap her? She needed a paper bag to breathe in.

"She put a Barrett M82A1 together in twenty-three seconds, and that was because she was hesitating at first."

Wilder whistled. "Well done, lady."

Yeah. She guessed so. "What about Peter Rainey?"

"That's where things get fun," Wilder said. "Peter Rainey doesn't exist. At least no one who matched the photo you sent. We called the rental car company. They weren't missing any vehicles but when they did a check at our insistence, they did find a tag stolen along with some rental papers. They checked their cameras and sent us footage, but this guy was good. No facial image. Nothing we could even use to ping off. But it's pretty obvious this Peter Rainey did it."

Grace's head might explode. What did this mean?

"Anything else?" Hollis asked.

"We ran a check on the make and model of the car. We found one reported stolen from a used car lot about seventy miles from Cottonwood," Wilder said.

Peter Rainey stole a car, stole a car tag and papers from a rental place which was pretty smart. If he was pulled over, he'd have the papers to match the license plate and the police would assume it was legit and not a stolen vehicle. "Thanks for all the help."

"No prob. If you need anything else, we're a phone call away."

They hung up and Hollis stared into the wind. He rubbed the stubble on his chin.

After several long beats, Grace couldn't stand it. Was he thinking the worst too? Would it change the way he felt about her—as a friend that is? Hollis didn't think of Grace romantically. "I'm going to clean out the storage shed." She rushed to the side of the building. Hollis didn't follow. He *was* thinking the worst. His good friend, sweet Grace who rescued little girls from the woods, quilted with a group of senior ladies, baked cookies with Tish and drank chamomile tea probably blew heads off human beings for cash—if she wasn't a sniper. But why would Colombians hunt down a military sniper? That made no sense. No… Grace had a sick feeling she wasn't the good guy at all.

She hauled open the shed door and the smell of river water smacked into her senses. A tiny crack of light pushed its way through the filthy window. As she weaved through the equipment, kayaks, canoes and paddles hanging on the walls, she made her way to the back. She didn't even know why she told Hollis she was coming to do this. The shed was in order and would never be spotless from dirt and cobwebs. She needed a minute to think. To process the information.

Hollis must have known that—or he was too overwhelmed and unable to find the words to come find her. It was a horrible situation and Grace might be a horrible person. Maybe she was overreacting. But if she'd been in a profession as docile as a kindergarten teacher, she wouldn't be in Bogota or know how to assemble a rifle. She searched Bogota on her phone. Capital of Colombia. Terrorists! Drugs!

Hairs on her arms rose but before she could turn, a rowing oar came around her neck and strong arms used it to pull her backward, choking her with the wooden paddle. She elbowed the attacker and instead of trying to move forward, she pressed into him, giving her some room to breathe. Grace shoved him into the kayaks stacked against the wall.

"I wasn't expecting too much of a fight," he said.

Challenge accepted. That same crazy sensation rushed over her and without thought, she twisted around, but he shoved her forward and pulled a gun. "You're going with me."

She stared at the gun, her heart slamming into her rib cage, but a memory bobbed on the edge of her consciousness. She lurched forward, disarmed him in two moves and rendered him useless. She grabbed the ropes hanging on the wall and went to work. Whoever this man was, he was going to talk. No matter what she had to do.

Hollis heard the commotion in the shed. Grace probably knocked the kayaks over like dominoes again. He headed that way to help her but his mind wouldn't let up on what he'd witnessed. She'd assembled that rifle like a pro. Like someone who had done it hundreds or thousands of times. He wasn't sure what it meant, but it unsettled him. Not to mention, she had a memory flash in her kitchen that she didn't want to share, one she tried to switch subjects about with hopes he'd forget, but he hadn't. He wouldn't. But Hollis wasn't one to press. He had memories he would rather not share too.

He heard another thud and picked up his pace. When he reached the shed, Grace had an oar to a man's neck and he was bound to a rickety chair.

"Who are you?" she asked with more force than he'd heard from her before.

The man in the chair was about Hollis's height. Two-eighty. Military haircut. Hardened ice-blue eyes and defiance all over his clean-shaven face. Maybe mid- to late-twenties.

"Grace?" When Grace turned her head, she had the look of a hungry wolf. Teeth bared, wild eyes. Who was this woman?

"What?" she demanded with an edge in her voice.

*A soft answer turneth away wrath.*

The proverb swept through his mind. "Hey," he whispered. "I just want to know what's going on. Are you all right?"

Suddenly it was like a fog cleared in her eyes. She dropped the paddle and backed away as if she'd terrified herself.

"Go ahead," the man said. "Do what you do best, lapdog. You won't get anything out of me." He laughed and Hollis assessed him. He was breakable. Still young. Tough. But he could be forced to talk. Hollis had no plans to try it. This wasn't war, but Grace's life was at stake. Had Hollis not shown up when he had, Grace may have tried to break the man, and she probably would have succeeded.

"I—I have no… I don't even—" Grace rushed from the shed, sprinting across the yard.

Hollis turned to Crewcut. "Why did you call Mad Max a lapdog? You know she does what she wants when she wants. Or are you the lapdog sent to fetch her? Never actually seen her up close have you?" Hollis grinned, hoping his acting skills worked. If he could use the nickname and pretend as if he knew who she was, then this guy might slip up and give him another clue. And if Crewcut knew she was a lapdog, and if doing what she did best implied—he swallowed—torture, then this kid had severely underestimated Grace, which made him stupid or he knew her only by reputation—Mad Max. Maybe.

"Max is as good as dead."

So he knew her nickname. Was it just Peter who called her that? Did this guy know Peter—or Peter's real identity? Had he been the one to kill him?

"You hear me, dead. Whether or not she gives us the doctor."

The temptation to throttle this guy was intense. He kept threatening Grace and no one was going to touch her. To keep his civility—even though this guy deserved a beating—Hollis exited the shed and chased after Grace. Then they'd figure out what to do with this guy. He wasn't going anywhere, considering Grace's skill with knots.

She stood by the water's edge at the creek, her arms folded as she rubbed her upper arms. "I don't know what happened. One minute I was terrified and fighting for my life and then it's like everything went dark. A switch flipped and before I realized it, I had him tied to a chair. I have no idea what I would have done had you not shown up." She faced him, tears in her eyes. "I think I'm a really bad person who's done unspeakable things."

Hollis closed the distance between them in three strides, pulling her to him in an embrace. "Grace, you don't know anything for sure and no matter what you did in the past, that's not who you are now. You're that new creation, remember? In Christ. I see the way you care about people and are kind. Whatever happened back there...that isn't who you are." But when her memories surfaced, she might want more than this simple small-town life regardless of who she'd been. She might have loved ones—a romantic loved one—who had been searching for her.

"I know who I feel like most days, but lately… I'm scared, Hollis. For my life. For what my past holds. I'm afraid for you. You didn't ask to be thrown into this. Your life is in danger by being associated with me. I couldn't bear it if something happened to you."

Warmth flooded him. Grace cared about him and his safety. That concern… He couldn't even remember the last time someone cared for him so tenderly. Not since Mom died. Tish—she was like a mom, but it wasn't the same. Grace… He couldn't go there. "You're a good friend, Grace. And friends help one another."

She pulled away and wiped her eyes with the sleeve of her long-sleeve T-shirt. "Yeah. Friends." She sniffed and pointed toward the shed. "What do we do with him? He isn't going to talk."

"He would. Eventually. If we did what it would take. But I'm not going to. And neither are you. Let's call Sheriff Freeman and he can decide." Cord would be more curious about how a woman who was five foot six and didn't come close to Crewcut's weight class had subdued the hefty dude. Hollis was frightened of her capabilities, and thoroughly impressed.

They entered the shed. Crewcut was gone. Somehow he'd gotten out of the ropes. Hollis's pulse pounded. "Get inside." They had no idea where he was or if he had weapons stashed nearby. Hollis pulled his weapon from his ankle holster and covering Grace, they sprinted inside the training facility. Grace paced Hollis's office.

"Do you think he's the guy who shot Peter? Who shot at us at the river?" She gnawed her thumbnail. She was an absolute mess.

"Maybe. I can't say for sure. But he didn't bat an

eye when I called you Mad Max." Hollis told her his conversation. "Which means he has some connection with Peter. I don't believe he's ever had personal contact with you before now. I wish I knew how the pieces fit." He'd give it another try. Hope she'd open up to him. Hollis couldn't blame her if she wanted to keep some of her memories private, but… "Grace, would you tell me about the memory you had when you dropped the coffee pot? It could be relevant."

She halted pacing and faced away from him. "I was with Peter. I think we may have been at a special event. He…he kissed me, and I was wearing an engagement ring."

Hollis's gut twisted. Grace and Peter more than likely had been a couple. Possibly engaged or married. All this time he'd been afraid she belonged to someone. Looked like to Peter. And she'd witnessed his murder. When her memories returned there would be grief even if Peter had betrayed her. "Do you know where you were in the memory?"

She refused to face him. Hollis slowly rounded his desk and laid his hands on her shoulders. "Grace, you are beautiful and bright. You were bound to have been in a relationship. I'm sorry you can't remember it, and I'm sorry you had to see him like that."

She finally turned. "You always know what to say. Always kind and thinking of others first. I wish I were that person."

He cradled her cheeks. "You are."

"I don't know, Hollis. What if I become that awful person again? What if I want to when—if—my memory comes back?" She covered her eyes with the heel of her hands. "What if I can't deal with everything I've done?"

He held her close and kissed the top of her head.

"You can choose who you want to be. And we don't know that you were a bad person. You could be a US Marshal. A soldier. A former soldier."

"Or I could be an assassin."

There was also that. But Hollis didn't want to go down that road or what it would mean when she had total recall. Because that would make her a criminal. A murderer.

And that would mean she'd have to go to prison.

# FOUR

After they had contacted Sheriff Freeman and waited on him to arrive to take more statements, Grace had sat at the kitchen table at the Muddy River Inn sipping a cup of hazelnut coffee with heavy cream and staring at the sunshiny walls.

Nothing inside felt sunshiny.

Outside the rain had continued to steadily fall. Hollis and Grace had checked the levee right after they finished with the sheriff. It was rising pretty fast. Hollis seemed to think it would hold—if the rain slowed in the next couple of days.

Didn't seem like it would. Not according to the National Weather Service radar. Grace had kept a close eye on it. Weather changes fascinated her. Had they always? Weather—while predictable most times—could change suddenly, and for the worst. Then as quickly become calm and peaceful. It reminded Grace of how fast her anger had set in when she'd been attacked. Like a wild rage. Where did that kind of temper come from? What had she done and whom did she hurt when it burst out of her in the past?

At the moment, she was anxious and afraid. Coffee probably wasn't the best choice. Tish entered the kitchen, a friendly smile but concerned eyes trained on Grace. "How are you feeling, hon?"

"Like a roller coaster of emotions."

"None of this is a surprise to God, you know." Tish poured herself a cup of coffee. "I don't know why He's allowing it. I don't know what good will come from it. But I do know that His Word says He works everything out for good," she touched Grace's hand, "for those who love and trust Him."

Grace did love God. And she did trust Him—to bring back her memory, to protect her now. Just seemed like He was a bit slow at the moment. She could have used her memories ages ago. "Thank you, Tish. I know Hollis feels like the inn is relatively secure—more secure than my own home because of how public it is, but you might be safer if I find somewhere else to stay."

"Nonsense. Hollis knows best. And family stick together—that's what we are in my eyes, Grace."

Grace wasn't sure what she'd do without Tish. Had Grace's mother loved her and cared for her like Tish was now? In her daydreams, she'd been part of a loving, happy family. She'd had a fluffy dog and even a horse. But who knew what Grace's childhood had been like. Why didn't her parents reach out to find her? Or had they? Were they?

The door opened and Hollis dripped on the welcome mat. "I have seen enough rain to last me a lifetime. How do people make it in Seattle?" He slipped off his raincoat and hung it on the hook by the door. After wiping his hiking boots on the mat, he headed straight for the coffee pot. "This smells like your foo-foo brew."

Tish snorted. "It's hazelnut and you're welcome to decline a cup." She winked at Grace and pushed open the door from the kitchen to the inn's dining area. "Let me know if you need anything else."

"You are the best, Tish."

"And don't you forget it." She clicked her tongue a couple of times and bustled into the dining area.

Hollis poured his cup and sipped. "Not bad."

"For foo-foo brew," she chuckled.

"The area is secure. I went over the details with Cord. He's going to have a deputy drive by every forty-five minutes to an hour. He even offered for you to bunk in his guest room." A divot formed in the middle of his brow. "Wasn't that nice of him?"

Grace hid her smile behind her mug. "It was. I guess you turned that offer down."

"I can protect you just fine. I don't think seclusion is smart at this point."

"I'm afraid causalities may arise if we stay in a public place." Whoever was after her wasn't going to stop.

"They don't seem to want to cause too much of a ruckus, minus dropping Peter Rainey in your home—but they kept to the shadows."

"One shot. Gone. Vanished." She had to agree on that point with Hollis. "I can't stay in the inn 24/7, though. If I'm stuck here, I'll feel caged, and somehow, I am certain that will not bode well for me. Or you."

Hollis raised an eyebrow and sipped his brew. "I believe you. We'll do what we can and be cautious. I think Cord will work with us—or you. And when we aren't trying to discover who is after you, we'll deal with this weather. If it floods…don't expect sleep anytime soon. We'll be rescuing folks—and even pets—left and right."

"Let's pray it doesn't come to that."

"I am. Believe me, I am."

Grace finished her cup and snagged a notepad off

the kitchen desk and a silver pen from Tish's rooster-shaped pen holder.

"Whatcha doin'?" Hollis asked.

"I'm going to write down what I do know." She scribbled her notes, which included two possible sets of people coming after her, the information she'd gleaned from Peter and her vague memory of him as well as who Dr. Sayer probably was based off what they'd learned from CCM.

Making a second column, she began listing the possibilities of Grace's identity. Soldier, former soldier, US Marshal, a protected witness, a doctor or someone in the medical field. Then she listed the more unsavory ideas.

Tish rushed into the kitchen. "Hollis! The downstairs bathroom is flooding. Can you come see about it?"

Hollis gulped his coffee and put his mug in the sink. "On it." He looked at Grace, his eyes darkened. "Go nowhere."

"Aye, aye, Captain," she said with a bite and saluted. She was used to taking orders from him with the search-and-rescue missions, why did this irritate her so much now?

Hollis squinted and opened his mouth to speak, but remained silent and followed Tish.

Hollis was trying to protect her. She huffed and a blip of a memory invaded her mind along with the scent of flowers. Grace was in a garden. A beautiful manicured flower garden with a large fountain.

"Hector, this is incredible," she said.

Her arm was tucked into a Latino man's. He was average height. Jet-black hair equally as dark as his eyebrows and eyes. Bronzed skin. Older than Grace by several—maybe many years—but he was handsome. Powerful. His deep voice reached her ears. "You are thrilling." He kissed her cheek, lingering. His phone rang and he answered. The sound on the other end was muffled, but Grace knew she'd been trying hard to listen.

His mouth straightened into a hard line. "Do nothing until I arrive. Don't tell her you've called me. I'll leave at once." He hung up, pocketed the cell phone.

His eyes darkened. "I'll be home in a couple of days. Go nowhere."

Grace's anger rose and nearly boiled over, resentful that she was forced to allow him to bark orders but also knowing it was dangerous not to obey him.

Why?

The memory was gone as quickly as it erupted. Hollis's identical words—his serious tone—must have brought it back and that misplaced frustration had been thrust at Hollis.

This was two memories so far and both involved men. Both felt romantic. What was going on? Who was Grace? Some kind of call girl or something? Grace might be keeping all kinds of secrets from dozens of people.

She swallowed and sat at Tish's desktop computer.

Maybe Grace could do a little digging on her own. She did an online search for the name Hector coupled with Bogota, Colombia.

Several headlines popped. Grace clicked on the first one and a picture morphed on the screen. The same man in her memory.

Hector Salvador.

Drug lord from Colombia. He'd been arrested two years ago in Hope, Tennessee, a small southern town. 'Bout the same time she'd been beaten up and gone into a coma. According to this news article, he'd come to the town to destroy a rival drug cartel. She continued to skim. His former sister-in-law lived in Hope…yada, yada, yada… Blair Sullivan…married the undercover DEA agent leading the investigation.

She did a little more digging. Blair McKnight now. Still lived in Hope. Ran a small antiques shop. Was she who had called him in that memory? Had he left Grace to go to Hope, Tennessee?

"All is fixed," Hollis said as he entered. Grace hurried and exited the screen, her stomach flopping around like a fish. "I'm sorry. I didn't mean to startle you." He approached her and laid a warm, gentle hand on her shoulder. "Whatcha doin'?" He glanced at the computer.

"Just trying to find out some stuff."

"Anything on Dr. Sayer?" he asked. Of course, he'd think she was searching for information on the doctor. Until Grace knew more about Hector and her relationship with him, she wanted Hollis in the dark. He'd already looked at her with what appeared to be fear in his eyes in the shed. Not fearful of her…but of who she might be. She'd read it loud and clear. He also knew she'd kissed Peter and might have been engaged to him. The last thing she wanted to admit was that she probably had some freaky torrid affair with the head of a powerful drug cartel!

Shame flamed her cheeks, turning them hot, and tears pricked her eyes. "Nothing on her." It wasn't a lie. Lying to Hollis—to anyone—seemed wrong on many levels. But Grace had a frightening feeling that she'd lied a lot in her past and never thought twice about it.

Hollis's gaze bored into her but he said nothing. When he crossed the room to the plate of cookies on the island, she let out a sigh of relief. False relief. There would be no real easy breathing until she was safe, her identity known and hopefully her past put to rest.

Right now her best option to help her accomplish these things was to find Hector Salvador—which wouldn't be difficult since he was in prison and that was no secret—and hope he could give her a few pieces to the puzzle, or a lot of pieces. But could a man like Hector be trusted?

Her second-best option was to call his former sister-in-law, Blair McKnight. According to the articles, she hadn't had contact with Hector, her late husband's brother, but that didn't mean Blair had never met Grace. And if she had zero knowledge of Grace, she still might have some useful information about Hector—like would he talk to Grace?

Grace almost died two years ago. The same time the doctor in Bogota went missing as well as when Hector went to the States and was arrested. The news said it was drug related and rival cartel related…but was it? Was there more there that the news media didn't know?

If Grace was involved with Hector's imprisonment, the last thing he'd do was tell her the truth. Based on the men coming after her…she was pretty sure she'd made an enemy out of the Colombian drug lord and he was vengeful.

He might come across the table and kill her himself.

Hollis sat across from Grace at the Muddy Brewhaha coffee café on Main Street, watching the rain slick down the window pane. The street had an inch of rain and car tires cut paths through the dirty water. Kali hummed behind the counter as she whipped up espressos, hot teas and served muffins to patrons who were trying to stay dry and caffeinated. Hollis had brought Grace for those same reasons and to coax her into telling him the truth.

He wasn't an idiot. Earlier today, Grace had been on that computer. And the second she'd excused herself to the bathroom, he'd checked the browser history.

Why was Grace searching for Hector Salvador? She'd obviously had a memory of him. He could be a link to her past—her identity. Hector Salvador was a deadly threat. He'd done his own research on him while Grace had helped Tish check in a couple of visitors and serve dinner to outside guests.

It was almost 7:00 p.m. But they were both restless. Hollis was a frenzy inside. He'd never been anything but honest with Grace, and up until now she'd never kept anything from him. At least that he was aware of. Should he tell her that he'd searched her browser history? Maybe he shouldn't have done it; it was her life— her privacy. He respected that immensely, and under normal conditions he'd have never even dared. Except this wasn't normal conditions and her life was in peril. Any sliver of information could give them a leg up. Yet, Grace had chosen to conceal information. Without it, Hollis couldn't fully protect her.

What was her relationship with Hector? The thought of a romantic one with a man like him sent shivers down Hollis's spine. The woman he knew now wouldn't even give it a thought. Maybe she'd been played by him…or she had worked for Hector Salvador in some capacity. But even then, it would be under less than noble conditions. The woman was schooled in guns and Hector Salvador was more than a powerful drug lord. He ran guns. Grace might have too—or even been one of his hired killers.

That look in her eye when she had Crewcut bound

in the shed. Arctic. No remorse for tying him up and what that implied.

But that wasn't the Grace Hollis cared about now. That wasn't his friend who sat with him at church and sang loudly, played board games with him on slow nights at the SAR facility or the same woman who loved to stitch a quilt.

His coffee was getting cold. Grace's maple pecan muffin remained untouched.

"You're quiet," he said as the rain pelted the roof and windows, coffee café music played lightly in the background and the scent of maple and cinnamon wafted through the atmosphere.

"Sorry," she muttered and stared out the pane as the gray evening turned black. "I'm not lively company tonight. I appreciate you getting me out of the inn, though."

She was going stir-crazy. Like himself. And he knew her well—at least the Grace here in the present. He studied her eyes, hair…she might have a touch of Hispanic descent in her. Could Hector be family? He was old enough to be an uncle—maybe her father—but Hollis couldn't be sure.

Grace fiddled with the locket she always wore. That thing wouldn't unlock and she didn't want to destroy it by cracking it open, only to see a possible picture of people she might not recognize. It was all she had of value when she was found. The way she'd kissed it before firing the rifle yesterday…like it was a ritual she had done often. Muscle memory.

But with new information, the subject of having it broken open might need to come up again. With so many snippets of memory, if there were photos inside, she might recognize them now. But he'd give her some time to process before dumping it on her.

"We needed a change of scenery. Probably should have ordered decaf, though."

She softly smiled, her eyes meeting his. Long dark lashes canopied hers. Sometimes, she stole his breath right out of him. Not just with a look, but with the way she was confident and yet vulnerable. The way she tackled new projects and wanted to attempt any- and everything. Her laugh. Low and throaty, and when she tossed her head—enough. Hollis stuffed all those emotions into a locked box marked Off-Limits. He needed it to stay as locked tight as Grace's locket.

"Probably," Grace responded. "Hollis?"

"Yeah," he murmured, hoping this was the moment she'd spill the beans, reveal what she knew about Hector Salvador. He braced himself for the worst-case scenario. No matter what, he could take it.

She searched his eyes and he watched as they dulled, then continued blankly staring out the window. "Never mind. I don't know what I was gonna say." She sighed and disappointment pinched his heart.

"You sure about that?" he asked. "I'm pretty tough. I can take whatever you might want to tell me. And not judge you." But he couldn't lie and say it wouldn't affect him. It would—at first. Then he could get past it. See the real, true Grace sitting in front of him. The Grace who rescued puppies and played peekaboo with toddlers in grocery lines. The question is how would it affect Grace?

Already it was sending her inside herself—like a caterpillar in a cocoon. Hollis couldn't be sure that when she finally emerged, she'd be a butterfly. But he wanted her to be.

"I'm sure. I'm tired. Let's go back to the inn. I need to try and sleep."

Rest might change her mind.

"Okay." He helped her into her raincoat and they said goodbyes to Kali and raced into the rain, rushing to his truck. He opened the door for her first, then hopped in the driver's side. "Drenched in thirty seconds."

The edges of his jeans were wet. He was thankful for waterproof hiking boots. Grace wore flowered rain boots, her jeans tucked inside.

He pulled onto Main Street, driving slowly. Didn't want to hydroplane or flood his truck. "Hey, can we run by my place real quick? If I'm going to stay at the inn, I need some extra clothes and I haven't had time to grab any for tomorrow. I badly need to do laundry."

Grace snickered at that. "Yeah, sure. I could do your laundry for you. I owe you that much."

He reached over and clasped her hand. "Grace, honey, you're terrible at laundry."

"I only turned my whites pink once. And so I occasionally shrink shirts…" She snorted. "You're right. Maybe you should do mine."

He laughed. Maybe he should but doing laundry felt a little more intimate than it ought to. "Pass. You did hear me say I'm terrible at getting mine done, right?"

"Yeah, I heard you."

He turned left off Main Street onto Old Highway 4 as if going toward the SAR facility. He lived about two miles down. Small ranch-style house on six acres. One day he was going to get a horse or two. The place already had the fencing. Needed a little mending is all. He pulled into his garage. "You wanna come in a minute?" Grace had been in his home dozens of times. Nothing new, but the pull on his gut was. Why was he nervous?

"Yeah." She hopped out and followed him inside the kitchen. He still had some dishes left in his sink. Papers, mail and an empty milk jug littered the counter.

"Sorry about the mess."

"No worries."

Hollis strolled from his kitchen toward the bedroom and called, "There's sweet tea in the fridge if you want some."

"I'm good," she hollered back.

His bedroom wasn't as cluttered as his kitchen. Old habits died hard. Bed made. Clothes put away. He hurried and tossed a bag together and threw it over his shoulder. As he reached the living room, Grace was perched on the brown leather sofa sifting through a fishing and wildlife magazine.

"Anything of interest?" he asked.

She raised her head and grinned. "No. Just passing time. I love your house."

Hollis laughed, but the words struck a chord in the marrow of his bones. "Yeah? What do you love about it?"

Shrugging one shoulder, she scanned the living room. "It feels like a home. Warm. Cozy. I love all the land. You should buy a couple of horses. Get a puppy," she murmured.

He'd had to put Bruiser—his German shepherd—down last February. He'd been a rescue dog, already several years old. Bruiser had been Hollis's best friend for the past four years. The house was quiet without him. "Maybe I will."

"It's peaceful out here. And gorgeous."

"Anything else? You want me to sell it to you?"

Grace stood and tossed the magazine on the coffee table. "Nah. I don't think it would feel quite so good if you weren't living in it." She held his gaze.

One beat.

Two.

Three.

She cleared her throat. Was she saying that he...*he* felt like home? No, he was reading more into it than necessary, but his pulse spiked and it felt like two horses were galloping through the pastures of his gut.

"Guess we ought to be going," he said. Sudden awkwardness replaced their quiet moment.

"Guess so." She followed him to the garage and into the truck. The garage door rose and he cranked the engine.

Rain continued to fall in a steady rhythm.

He backed out of the drive as a bullet slammed into the tailgate.

Hollis shifted gears and hit the gas, reentering the garage, then he punched his finger on the garage opener clipped to his visor.

Grace had already crouched low and retrieved his Glock from his console. "One in the glove box too," he said as a bullet pierced the bumper right before the garage door closed and sealed them inside.

Grace chambered a round, handed off the gun to Hollis, then opened the glove box and snatched the SIG Sauer as she slid from the truck.

"In the house," Hollis commanded and they rushed into the kitchen. "Stay down."

"Be careful," Grace said. While her demeanor seemed cool as lemonade on a summer day, her voice quivered.

He paused while hunched down, using the cabinets as a shield and lightly touched her hair. "Don't worry. You sit tight."

She nodded and he stayed low. The house was dark.

Most of the blinds closed. They had an advantage. Unless the shooter had night-vision goggles. Seemed too far-fetched, but the way this had been playing out so far, Hollis wasn't taking any risks. He slipped through the kitchen to the breakfast area and put his back against the wall, slowly peeking out the window. Too much rain blurring his vision. Hollis couldn't be sure where the shooter might be at this moment. A good sniper had taken out Peter Rainey. Hollis had no clue how far the shooter could pick them off from. Depended on skill.

Dropping to his stomach, he belly-crawled into the living room. "Grace, you okay?"

"I'm good. You?"

He peeped out the living room windows that faced the north side of the house. "Right as rain, honey." Scared out of his mind that something might happen to her.

"Can you see anyone? Anything? Movement?"

"No. Unfortunately."

A bullet shattered the breakfast area window; the sound of rain grew louder. "We gotta move, Hollis. Now. Out the front."

But…

"What if there's more than one shooter?" He couldn't risk her going out the front and getting picked off. Whoever had come for her could be herding her to her death. Hollis wouldn't play into the possible game.

Grace slithered into the living room. Gun in hand. Fire in her eyes but also fear. Fear was a great motivator. Also, could cause irrational decisions.

"Fine, let's go out a side window. If they're playing us to the opposite side, why give them the satisfaction?"

Hollis licked his lip as another shot came through the door.

"What if someone out there knows you? Knows the way you think. What if how you are thinking now is exactly how you would think then? They'll expect you to do the unexpected. And they'll be waiting."

The fire in her eyes quickly cooled. Hollis didn't want to scare her, but he didn't want to make a rash move. He wanted to protect her and get them somewhere safe. That was what he was trained to do. It's what he would do.

"I don't know then," she stammered. "But we're nothing but targets in here."

Too much glass to crawl through the kitchen again.

Another shot blew out the living room window. The shooter had shifted position. "Let's go!"

They stayed low and rushed to the guest bedroom off the hall on the west end.

"I'll go first," Hollis said. "Make sure it's secure."

"And if it's not, you're dead." Terror pulsed in Grace's eyes.

"But you're not. No arguments." He raised the window and before she could protest, he jumped into the bushes. Grace followed suit.

A bullet hit the top of the window, spraying bits of brick off the house.

"We're cornered!" Grace shouted.

And blind in the rain.

They might not make it out of this one.

# FIVE

Rain drenched Grace's head, matting her hair to her cheeks. Drops of water slid onto the collar of her shirt.

She and Hollis crouched behind the bush but any second another bullet would hit them. "Our best chance is the woods across the street. Nothing but pastureland behind us. Too wide open," Hollis whispered.

"Agreed."

Grace's hand shook, but she steadied the gun. Mustered the courage. They were ripe for the picking.

"When I fire, run," Hollis said, his voice raspier than normal.

He rose up and fired a couple of rounds and Grace sprinted from the bushes, keeping low and to the side of the house. A bullet struck the gutter above her head and she returned fire. Hollis was right behind her.

Once they got to the front of the house, they darted to the large sweetgum tree.

Nothing but rain fell.

No sound of gunfire.

But they weren't out of danger.

They had about fifty feet to make it across the muddy road and into the woods beyond. "On my count," Hollis said and cupped Grace's cheek. "You run and you don't look back. No matter what."

What did that mean? "You run with me."

"I'll be behind you. But you run and don't stop. Understand?"

She nodded, but her bottom lip trembled.

"One...two...three!"

Hollis fired in the direction the shots had been coming from.

Grace tore out from behind the tree, racing across the lawn, her rain boots kicking up mud and water as she set her sights on the woods ahead.

A bullet hit the mud puddle two feet from her.

Hollis's gun fired again. "Keep going!"

Grace desperately wanted to look back. To check on Hollis. Make sure he was safe and directly behind her. Guns continued to fire.

Five feet...four...

She flew into the shelter of the trees. Her calves burned, her lungs ached but she pushed through not even sure where she was running. Finally, it grew quiet. Nothing but rain pelting the fresh green leaves and the sound of her breathing.

Backing into an evergreen for cover, she listened.

No footsteps.

No voice.

No gunfire.

Her heart leaped into her throat. Where was Hollis? He said he'd be right behind her, but she'd been running for a while. What if one of those bullets had hit him? He could be lying in his yard—the peaceful patch of land that always made Grace feel at home. A place she'd just stated needed him to feel that way. She needed him; he was like the center of gravity for her.

Not only to get her through the tough times. She needed his strength. His laughter that always filled her with joy. She needed his quick wit and his soft prayers.

Grace couldn't hide and do nothing while her best friend in the world might be injured. Leaving him wasn't an option.

She moved through the darkness, using the trees as cover—listening and going on instinct. As if she'd had to become a ghost before. Blending with shadows. Moving like night. Becoming one with the forest. Even her footsteps seemed lighter, quieter.

Another ripple of terror rocked through her. How... why could she move like this?

She made it about ten feet from the tree line when a hand fell on her shoulder. In a swift move, she twisted, flipping the attacker over her back and onto the ground. She placed a boot on his neck and aimed her gun.

"Grace! It's...me...put a cork in the creature of the night!" Hollis's voice was strained from her foot on his throat. Grace released him.

"Good way to get shot, Hollis," she groused. "Have you lost your mind?"

He jumped to his feet, turning his nose up. "My back is sopping wet. Thanks to you."

"Me—the creature of the night? Hmm?"

He finally stopped scowling long enough to sheepishly grin, but it didn't last long. He glanced at Grace and her position. "I know you run faster than this."

Busted.

"I didn't know where you were. Or if you were hurt. So..." She shrugged.

"You were coming for me?"

She didn't want a lecture or a reprimand. A hint of a memory teetered on the edge of her mind. Like she'd been here before. Ignoring commands. But that was all it was. A feeling. A sensation.

"I'm not sorry either," she laid on the defiance pretty thick. "So save the rant."

Hollis sighed. "I held him off as long as I could then went the other way, hoping to confuse him. Then I ran straight for where you ought to be. You weren't there."

"Nope." She jutted out her chin.

He lightly clipped it with his knuckles and smirked. It did a wild dance inside her. "No," he whispered, "you were too busy trying to rescue me. I don't know how to feel about that."

"I hope not sexist."

Hollis laughed but quickly contained it. Clasping her cheeks in his calloused, wet but warm hands he placed a big ole kiss to her forehead. "No, not sexist." He ran his thumb across her jawline. "I mean, part of me hates it because well...you're my favorite. If anything ever happened to you—even more so because of me—I don't know what I'd do. The other half of me is not only impressed as all get-out, but proud of you. Ready to fight beside you. Not just for you."

His words tore through her, settling into hollow crevices, warming her entire body, flooding her heart. She was his favorite. He was hers too. "So, you know why I came back then."

Inky eyes searched hers and her pulse skittered as he stepped into her personal space and his lips descended toward hers, his intentions clear.

But before he connected with her, the thought of being someone else's favorite swept through her. She might have been Hector Salvador's favorite. Peter Rainey's. Who knew who else?

Shame was left in those horrific thoughts' wake.

She broke away from his gaze, his touch and stepped a few feet away. Pushing down her feelings, she faked a cordial smile. "I mean I don't have a friend as good as you. And I always beat you in Battleship, so I'd hate to see harm come to you, leaving me to find a new friend to play games with."

A minuscule pop of pain crossed his face, but he nodded. "You are difficult to be around. You may not find another friend."

And like that, the moment was over.

That might be the real tragedy tonight. But Grace wasn't in a place to make a shift in their relationship. She wasn't even sure it was more than two close friends almost dying and sharing a moment of serious gratitude.

"You sure he's gone?" Grace asked. Leaving the wooded fortress might be a bad idea.

"No. But we can't sit here all night." Lights shone up ahead and Grace gripped Hollis's shirt.

"It's okay. It's Cord."

Sheriff Freeman's SUV rolled to a stop and he lowered the passenger window. "Miss Ellerby called, said lots of gunfire was going off near your place. Thought I might check it out with what's been transpiring. Looks like I'm right," he said with a mild sour note to his voice. "Unless you just enjoy hanging out in the woods during a thunderstorm."

Hollis jumped in the passenger seat and Grace climbed in, scooching down just in case. Sheriff Freeman eyed the two them. "Everyone in one piece?"

"I think so. Thank you, Sheriff."

"Cord. You can call me Cord." He peered in the rearview mirror and smiled. Friendly. Nothing more.

Grace returned it. "What now?"

"Now, we get you safe and dry," he said.

Hollis peered out the passenger window, his elbow on the door and his fist under his chin. Grace wasn't sure if he was thinking about the shooter or the almost kiss. A kiss that could not happen. Surely, he knew that. She had no past. Nothing to offer. What she did have was sketchy at best. Downright criminal at worst.

"Dry and safe sounds amazing." She glanced at Hollis's house. "You left your bag of clothes."

"I can wash these at Tish's." His voice seemed far off. Even Cord stole a peek and frowned. "Why don't y'all stay with me tonight? I have an extra set of clothes. I don't like putting you two and others in danger at the inn."

"Fine." Hollis didn't even argue. He'd been pretty certain the inn would be safe. Guess he changed his mind.

"Well, if anyone wants my opinion, I'm fine with that, too, but I'd like to get some of my own clothes."

Cord chuckled. "Yeah, my stuff will hang off you."

Hollis shot Cord a withering glare. "She'll wear her own clothes. We'll stop at Grace's first." From distant to on fire. Well, she'd rather have him hot than cold.

Cord drove to Grace's little home and parked. Hollis opened the door. "I'll come inside with you." He opened Grace's door since it was locked from the inside and helped her out, then they walked in silence to the front door. Grace unlocked it and Hollis went inside first.

Once he secured it, she headed into her bedroom, but he caught her arm. He looked absolutely tortured.

All because of her.

"I'm sorry, Grace. For what I almost did in the woods. I have no business kissing you and you had every right to pull away. Forgive me?"

There was nothing to forgive. But he clearly regretted it. Is that why he'd seemed distant then fired up in the SUV? Was her past becoming a wedge between them? Was the probability that she was more criminal than hero a factor?

What if she got her memory back and had to go to prison? The terror struck her rigid.

"What's wrong, Grace?"

"I'm just tired. Let me get a bag packed." She entered her room, but left the door cracked. Hollis gave her some privacy. She needed to know more, and as soon as she could get a free moment, she was going to call Blair McKnight and meet with her and her husband. If Hector Salvador could—and would—unlock her past, she was going to face him.

No matter the cost.

The rain had slacked, but the thunder continued to rumble in the distance. Hollis leaned against the kitchen counter as Cord made a pot of coffee. It was almost 10:00 p.m. and too late for caffeine. Hollis's nerves couldn't take any more zing.

Grace had retired to the guest room on the far end of Cord's modern farmhouse. Seemed awful big for a bachelor. Who was Hollis to judge, though? The kitchen filled with the scent of dark roast.

"She really okay?" Cord asked and eased into a wooden kitchen chair.

Good question. "I don't know. Would you be?"

"Unlikely. I looked into the Covenant Crisis Management team you told me about on Monday. My sisters, Teddy and Toni, are good friends with Wilder Flynn, and they both say he and his company are legit. They've done some contract work for him in a stalking case."

Cord crossed an ankle over his knee and toyed with the salt shaker on the table.

Hollis refrained from an eye roll. As if he'd let some sketchy private security company handle Grace's case—her life.

"What's your theory?" Cord asked. "The one you don't tell her?" The coffee pot beeped and Cord opened the cabinet and retrieved a mug with the marine corps crest.

"I don't know."

Cord smirked and a slight laugh escaped his nose in a single puff. "Yeah. You do." He poured a cup and returned to the kitchen table. Sipped the black brew. "Based on what you've updated me with—and I thank you for being forthcoming—I'm thinking our Grace Thackery did some very naughty things for hire. I think she got caught, and to keep out of prison, she flipped. Maybe for the DEA. Maybe FBI. ATF. I don't know."

Hollis had the same thought. With each new piece of information, his theory changed. No longer was she a victim of domestic violence. That no longer held water since her defense skills weren't average but lethal. Not to mention the way she handled a sniper rifle.

Cord thanked him for being forthcoming, but Hollis had refrained from informing him about Hector Salvador. Based on Cord's assumptions—Grace may have turned on Hector. When the authorities descended, they helped Grace and Dr. Sayer escape and put them into witness protection. Clearly, something went wrong. Dr. Sayer went missing and Grace got the stuffing beat out of her and went into a coma.

So where were the marshals? They would have looked through missing persons photos and found her already. Relocated her. Hmm...

Cord slurped his coffee. "Whoever she was collecting evidence against must have found out. Whupped her good and left her for dead, but why here? Why in Mississippi?" He set his mug down. "WITSEC. She must have been coming here to settle into a new life and whoever was after her caught up and left her for dead." He folded his arms. "And now they know she survived. Peter Rainey—or whoever he really was—might have been her marshal."

Made sense as to why the marshals hadn't come— they had. But if Peter didn't check in with them, they would have sent someone else. Could there be a marshal on the take? It wasn't a stretch.

"He did tell her that he was sorry for betraying her. That he could help her and something was all lies. He might have been duped into the betrayal and was trying to make amends, get her out and settle her somewhere else—maybe against his superiors' knowledge if one of them were involved in her near death. But they found out anyway and sent the guy I call Crewcut to take out Peter and get information from Grace." And then kill her. Or kill her either way. They sure seemed to want to tonight.

But a piece of the puzzle didn't fit—the memory of Grace on Peter's arm, the ring and his kiss. Could she have been involved with Hector Salvador and fallen in love with her marshal? Stranger things had happened. Even though it was against policy and Peter could've lost his job for it. But if the old Grace was anything like the new Grace, Hollis had to admit that losing a job would be worth it. "If this theory is true, she has immunity, which means she won't do prison time."

"All nice conjecture," Grace said as she entered the kitchen, dressed in a too-big sweatshirt and yoga pants.

For a second Hollis thought she might have taken Cord up on wearing his clothes—at least his shirt. Cord's earlier statement had ignited a frenzy of green in his blood. But he'd let it go. Hollis had no claims to Grace.

He'd misinterpreted their moment in the woods; she'd dodged his advance. A dumb move on his part. Hollis had lost his head; thinking too much with his heart. Hearts were deceiving. According to the Book of Jeremiah, the most deceitful and wicked. And Hollis was deceiving himself. Kissing her would only hurt him because he wouldn't be satisfied with just a kiss. Emotionally he'd want more. More of her. More of them. Grace wasn't able to give him anything else. And even if she was, Hollis wasn't willing to take that chance with his heart.

Grace strode to the coffee pot, hair in a sloppy bun on her head, not a stitch of makeup. Light purple circles sagged below her eyes. These past twenty-four hours had taken their toll. "You do think I was a criminal."

Hollis's neck heated. He'd been affirming over and again that she was probably a soldier. But now his other thoughts were out there. No denying them. Grace had probably been listening the whole time. "You might have been. Doesn't mean you are now."

Cord stood. "You were obviously doing the right thing by flipping and getting the bad guy if that's what went down."

Grace poured a cup and nailed Cord with an icy glare. "By getting caught. Isn't that what you said? Caught doing naughty things for hire? I do hope you mean hits and not things of ill repute." He'd never seen Grace so defensive and biting. Except once today— earlier when he'd told her to go nowhere and she'd saluted him with a sneer. He'd let it pass. Couldn't begin to imagine the kind of stress she was under. She was fighting in a war completely blind.

"I did not mean anything of ill repute, Grace," Cord said. "I meant hits, and I'm sorry if that upsets you, but we have to look at all the possibilities so we can sniff out the right trail. Hunt it. Fix it. Get closure."

Grace half laughed, half snorted. "Cord, until I have my memories, I'll never have closure. Doesn't matter if someone is trying to end me or not. That's just the straw on the camel's back."

"I don't mean to sound insensitive."

She motioned to his mug with her chin. "Semper fi. You're thinking like a soldier."

Hollis and Cord traded glances. Grace must have caught on. "I must have heard that phrase somewhere."

Or it was embedded in her memory and had surfaced when she laid eyes on the marine corps crest. Could she have been a marine? Hollis wanted so badly for Grace to have been honorable. For her sake. She'd been so worried about being a bad guy, about doing horrific things. If her memory came back, revealing what she feared most… How would she handle it?

Cord only nodded once. Keeping his thoughts close to the vest. "Do we have a game plan?" he asked. "I don't like playing defense. I'd much rather go offensive."

Hollis agreed. Unfortunately, they had no offense right now. Other than Hector Salvador. And Grace was playing him close to the vest too.

Grace poured another cup of coffee, added a splash of milk. The woman had a serious affinity for caffeine. She'd be up all night; maybe that's how she wanted it. "The team at CCM are working on it and have more resources and capabilities than us. What can we do that they can't?"

"Nothing." Hollis frowned. That was the part he hated. Doing nothing. Unable to.

"We can talk about this weather," Cord said, shifting gears. "It's not a killer…yet. But that levee is high and we already had flash flooding on Main Street. Fields are rising with water. Yards. Dyer Crawling has had his plumbing crew out all day long. I think we should sandbag some areas."

Hollis nodded. "I've already been thinking that. We can get started on it tomorrow morning. I'll put a group text out to volunteers. See who can make it."

"I'll lend some deputies. If it keeps rising, residents in flood zones will have to evacuate. Some already have as a precaution. If it doesn't let up, it'll ruin our Memorial Day picnic in town square."

The Memorial Day picnic was an annual event the entire town looked forward to. Potluck, patriotic decorations, live music and a special slide show tribute on the big outdoor screen of all the fallen heroes who had lived in Cottonwood.

"I can't remember the last time it rained like this," Cord mused. He'd lived here much longer than Hollis. Hollis had moved here only when the paid SAR Director position opened up. He'd finished his tours and wanted to settle down. Make a life. And he had. He loved Cottonwood, the people, his job.

"I can obviously help," Grace said, "when I finish up with Tish—unless she can handle breakfast and prepping lunch alone."

Hollis would prefer Grace stayed under his watchful eye. While he didn't think they'd be attacked publicly at the inn, he couldn't be sure a direct assault and attempt wouldn't be made. For a woman who had no memory, anyone could be an enemy.

\* \* \*

Grace awoke to gray rainless skies—for now. Later, she'd track the storm systems and help Hollis prep with sandbags. Last night's titillating conversation about how big of a criminal Grace might have been solidified her decision and when she'd retired to her room, she'd made the phone call to the analyst at CCM and obtained Blair McKnight's phone number.

She'd also mentioned to Wheezer to keep their conversation on the down low. Until she verified her connection with Hector Salvador, there was no point relaying that memory to Hollis.

Grace had intended to make the call to Blair and Holt McKnight this morning, but she'd been too antsy and had done it late last night. Holt had answered. After apologizing for the middle of the night phone call, she explained why she'd done it.

They'd been gracious to offer to meet her today and help in any way they could. They had welcomed her to come to Hope, but Grace couldn't escape Hollis long enough to go secretly, so she asked if they'd be willing to come to her.

Hollis's midmorning and afternoon would be filled sandbagging around the levee. Cord had promised to station a deputy at the inn to assuage Hollis's nerves since Grace needed to do her job at the inn.

She'd give the deputy the slip and meet them in private. Keeping secrets felt slimy. Hollis had always been open with her, but the overwhelming shame tied her tongue. Especially after overhearing Cord and Hollis discuss theories on her past—on who she'd been.

All of Hollis's positive talk to soothe her had been well and good, but the reality was he suspected she was every bit of a terrible person as she did. No one could blame him. But if the McKnights coughed up further nasty details about Hector, Hector and Grace's relationship or Grace in general, then the last thing she wanted was Hollis to hear every detail. Eventually, Grace would have to confide the possible new information—but she could give him an outline, not every sordid detail Blair or Holt might divulge.

A knock on her door drew her from her thoughts. "Grace? You 'bout ready?" Hollis asked.

"Yeah." She zipped her bag and opened the door. Hollis loomed in the doorway, scruffy from lack of shaving, hair a little disheveled, but he smelled like a fresh shower and toothpaste. Mercy, he was handsome. A bit sinister looking himself—when he wasn't shaved.

"You hungry?"

"No. I'll eat something at Tish's." Until she left to meet the McKnights at a tiny diner outside Cottonwood. Too risky meeting in town where rumors would reach Hollis's ears. *Lord, forgive me for the deception.*

Cord met them at the front door. "Offer stands to stay here. Between the two of us, you'll be safe, Grace. We've got you. Nobody you can trust more."

Something about those words...

*...got you...nobody you can trust more...safe...*

The ball of fury began as a fist in her abdomen then traveled like fire through her blood.

*...nobody you can trust more...*

Unable to recall a full conversation or the speaker behind the words. But the rage...the pure unadulterated rage tore through her and like lightning it snapped! Grace stepped into Cord's personal space, undaunted by his frame—the power behind it—as if she was fully aware she could snap him like a twig. She thrust a finger into his face. "I don't need you to take care of me," she fumed. "I have been taking care of myself a long time and believe me, I do a pretty good job."

Cord raised a dark eyebrow. "Okay."

Hollis laid a hand on Grace's shoulder and she bristled as if at any minute she'd need every single muscle in her body to protect herself. "Grace?" he asked softly.

His soothing tone, his gentle voice pulled on that rope of rage that had lassoed Cord…lassoed her own faculties—every part of her. It was uncontrollable and frightening.

"Grace, come on back to me now." His whisper reached her heart. Cooled the fury and the pain that seemed to ignite it. "And if ya see fit, maybe take your finger out of Cord's face."

Grace blinked and focused on Hollis—the fiery dart dislodged from her mind. "I'm sorry." She stepped away, shame replacing her anger. "I'm not sure why I said that." But it must have been in the recesses of her mind—it felt true. Had Grace been on her own—alone—before her incident? The edges of her faculties blurred as if wanting to conjure a memory but it remained hostage. "I really am sorry," she said. "Thank you for allowing me to stay here." She rushed out and slogged down the sidewalk to Cord's SUV.

Hollis swaggered toward her, a lopsided smirk on his face. Mischief in his eyes. "You do a pretty good job taking care of yourself, do ya? You put yourself in that coma? I mean—" he splayed his hands to his sides "—I suppose that makes sense, beating yourself senseless just to hide out from bad guys in the hospital. Get enough R & R?" He cocked his head.

Hollis had a way of taking a tough and awkward situation and diffusing it by making light of the heaviness. It worked every single time. She held in her grin and dusted invisible lint from his shoulder. "Best sleep of my life. So good I woke up and forgot who I was."

"That is some serious snoozing. I may be willing to beat the snot out of myself for that kind of sleep," he teased and opened the door.

"I could aid you in that knocking around. I have a feeling I'm quite adept at it." That part wasn't nearly as humorous. None of it was, but when Hollis teased like this—even over such a somber circumstance—it made her feel like the world wasn't so bad. Like Grace wasn't so vile. Like everything would work out for good and be okay.

"Well, you did a bang-up job on yourself."

She laughed and it soothed her soul, eased her tense neck muscles and gave her a small break from the severity of her reality. Hollis playfully clipped her chin with his knuckles—something he'd been doing since she warmed up to him after the coma.

He hadn't once turned his back on her. But someone had—she knew it deep down. Maybe more than one someone. Tears sprang to her eyes as she sobered at the thought. "Why are you so good to me?" She didn't deserve it.

"Why are you so good to me?" he countered.

Easy. "Because you're a good man." He could have easily taken advantage of her over the past year and a half, but he'd been noble, kind. Caring. Patient.

She climbed into the back seat.

Hollis leaned in, getting right up in her face. "And you, Grace Thackery, are a good woman." He brushed his thumb over her cheek, holding her captive with only his eyes.

If that were only true. "We both know I'm probably not." She dropped her head. He could go ahead and

say she was a new person now—but he had no idea
that she was presently deceiving him and withholding
information. If that had been the old her, then it was
cropping up in the new. That must mean she hadn't
changed. Not at all.

The idea terrified her. She didn't want to be the
woman it appeared she had been. She wanted to be
better.

Wiping a tear, he lifted her chin. "I know no such
thing."

Cord cleared his throat. "Y'all ready?"

Hollis closed the door and climbed in the front. Cord
slid into the driver's seat and cranked the engine.

They drove in silence until Cord broke it. "So, Grace,
what are you bringing to the Memorial Day picnic?"

Not quite the mood lightener as Hollis, but she admired that he was trying. Cord was attractive and kind.
More rigid than Hollis. But it was hard to compare any
man to Hollis Montgomery. Not a single one could hold
a candle.

She'd go with his path of conversation, though.
"Probably pasta salad."

Hollis flipped the visor down, opened the mirror
and peered at her through it—a twinkle in his eyes.
"If she has time in between picking off people with a
sniper rifle and trying to survive murderous attempts
on her life."

Grace caught the horror-stricken look on Cord's face
in the rearview mirror. She busted a gut. Hollis joined
in.

Finally, Cord smirked. "Ah, I get it. Inappropriate
joking is your thing."

It was. They had a thing. She kinda liked that. No,
she loved it. "And pasta salad," Grace added.

Hollis shifted in his seat and winked at her. "And pasta salad," he repeated. It wasn't so much the words but the emotion behind them, the way he held her gaze. It was as if she were looking into what their future could be—if there was a future to be had between them. Unfortunately, there wasn't. And who knew? Grace could be reading into his eyes, his gentle tone. Wishing when in truth it was simply a joking "thing" between friends.

After picking up Hollis's truck, he drove Grace to Tish's. "Stay close. I don't want to leave you here at all. It's a risk. But they did wait until we were alone in my house to attack. I'm hoping that was strategic and they are shying away from attacking in a public place. Just use common sense."

As if she planned to be stupid. "What's that?" she asked as she hopped out of the truck. "I can't remember."

He poked his head out of the window. "Now is not the time to make jokes, Grace."

She tipped her head, keeping a somber face. "I'm not. I can't recall the word."

Hollis squinted and studied her. "It means stay away from windows, don't go outside alone, don't clean rooms without Tish with you—safety in numbers... Don't take candy from strangers..." He flashed a wicked grin. "Eat all your vegetables."

"You knew I was kidding?" She thought she had him.

"I know you, Grace, and your facial expressions. Now get. I'll call and check in when I can and be back around one or one thirty—unless you need me before then."

She curtsied and heard him laugh as she hurried inside the inn's kitchen. He honked his goodbye and she grinned.

Tish looked up from stirring a pot of her famous marinara sauce. "You look like my Andrea when she came home from her first date with Mac."

Tish's daughter and Mac had been married for ten years. They lived near Memphis. Grace had met her many times. "I assure you I've been on no dates. Unless running for your life next to someone counts."

Tasting a spoonful of sauce, Tish grunted. "Running from love seems to me."

Pfft. "Am not." She lifted a pale blue apron off the hook and slipped it on, tying it around her waist.

"If you say so." She harrumphed and rinsed the spoon. "I'm making lasagna tonight. Should be easy enough. Easier than running from love, anyway."

Grace opened the fridge and frowned. "I'm not running from love. Hollis and I are friends, Tish." She grabbed the eggs, mozzarella cheese and ricotta and set them on the island. "I got zero to offer."

"Baloney."

"You want to put bologna in the lasagna?" she teased.

"You know exactly what I mean. Don't use that memory loss when it suits you, dear one. Like, to avoid falling in love with Hollis because you're afraid if it shattered to pieces, you'd be lost."

Grace grabbed her mixing bowl and began cracking eggs for the filling. "Not true." But it might be. She'd never let herself think about anything romantic with Hollis—at least for long. "But you're right about feeling lost without him. Hollis is my favorite."

"Mmm-hmm."

"As in my best friend. It's one thing to know about my past—if it's horrific—as a friend. But to be romantically involved… That might be too much to take. A friend could be supportive. A man in love with me, well, it might be enough to scare him away."

"So you say." Tish gave her a motherly scowl. "I've never seen Hollister Montgomery shy away from anything that might be overwhelming or frightening."

"I have to run an errand around ten."

"With Hollis?"

Grace didn't want to lie to Tish. But Hollis couldn't know about her appointment with the McKnights. "Santa. The president. Old Man Winter..." She laid on the sarcasm until Tish snorted. Her answers were so preposterous it had to be Hollis. Except it wasn't and Grace hadn't technically lied.

But she'd been deceptive and it had come easily. She shuddered and told herself it was for the greater good. More facts. Better handle on the situation and solving it. Then everyone was safe, including Tish.

After finishing the cheese filling for the lasagnas, she tossed her apron and peeked outside. Ugh. Rain again. But Tish was upstairs so now was a good time to go before any more questions arose and forced Grace to lie. She grabbed a raincoat by the kitchen door and her purse, hopped in her car and drove to the diner outside of town.

The greasy spoon smelled of onions and fried goodness. Not too crowded. Grace scanned the little establishment. In a corner booth, she recognized the pretty brunette as Blair McKnight from the news photos, and sitting beside her was a real live Superman, with eyes so blue they popped from here. Must be former DEA agent and her husband Holt. Swallowing fear, she made her way over.

"Mr. and Mrs. McKnight?" she asked.

"Grace?" Blair said.

Grace nodded and they finished making introductions as Grace took the open seat across from them.

Holt took the reins and recapped their conversation from the night before to make sure they understood everything. Grace nodded and revealed her fears. "I'd love to believe I'm not the bad guy. But everything is pointing to it. Even if I did flip on Hector. Would he tell me the truth about who I am—who I was?"

Blair glanced at her husband and he nodded once. She reached across the table and laid a hand over Grace's. "I'm sorry for what's happened and what you'll have to wade through if—or when—your memories return. Hector is a dangerous man with a powerful reach. His empire still flourishes under his control, even in prison. It sounds like you—and Dr. Sayer—betrayed him. That is one thing Hector does not tolerate. But she must be useful to him. Enough he wants her back alive and has likely been searching for her these past two years."

Holt rubbed his dark scruffy chin. "And he wants you to spill her location. I think the attempts on your life—at least the ones under his authority—may be to scare and even wound you, but not kill you. You're valuable to him at the moment as well."

After they found Dr. Sayer, Grace would be expendable. Then he would come full force like the other people who had tried to kill her. She was doomed. "Why do you think he wants the doctor?"

Holt leaned forward, tenting his fingers on the table. "I did some digging after we talked. Made some phone calls. According to my friends at the DEA, Hector had a private lab on his compound—if I wasn't undercover in Hope working on finding a missing agent I would have known about the lab and maybe have been on the team that descended on the compound when it appears you fled with the doctor."

Missing agents. Missing doctors. Felt like an action movie.

Holt continued. "When the DEA infiltrated the compound, the lab was already ablaze. They detained the remaining four scientists on-site—all mid- to late-twenties. They testified that Patsy Sayer employed them to work on a project in conjunction with the CDC—"

"Let me guess. That wasn't true."

"No. She told them their research was top secret and because the assignment was above their pay grade, they were given only bits and pieces of information on a need-to-know basis to conduct the project."

"Did they have any inkling what that project might be?" Grace asked.

"They all agreed it was a toxin. One young man in the group believes now—after the DEA showed up— that it was all lies and Hector Salvador was going to use the toxin to crop dust over his rival cartels' poppies, wrecking their harvest."

"Poppies? Sorry, my memory…"

"Poppies are gathered to make opiates—drugs. Which means Hector would rule the drug trade."

Grace pinched the bridge of her nose. "According to our sheriff's theory, I was at the compound collecting evidence for a government agency. If that's true, I must have been after information on the toxin. But if the lab was on fire when the DEA arrived and all the information burned…did I double-cross the agents or did something else happen? If I was responsible for it, did I plan to do something sinister with the information? That could be why I ran and took the doctor. And who tipped them off that Hector was off-site? The DEA came when he was out of the country, right?"

"They didn't know about the toxin—they did know about a lab. They assumed from surveillance it was for opiates. The reason they came when they did was because they got news Hector had been arrested in Hope. It was a prime opportunity. Confiscate drugs. Arrest his cronies. Add to his charges. How you and the doctor escaped and you ended up in Mississippi is a mystery I have no hypothesis on," Holt said.

Grace sipped the water the server had brought and racked her brain, begged it to produce a memory. "If Hector wants Dr. Sayer, then he may want her to finish the toxin or give him the compounds and research. Right?"

"Yes. He's probably been searching for her this entire time. You said this Peter guy saw you on the news, right? It was national? Likely," Holt said, "Hector, or one of his men, saw you too."

Grace had more questions than answers. "Is there anything else you know that might help me?"

Holt and Blair exchanged glances.

Holt sighed. "Grace, you should know that the scientists stated Hector had a mistress living on the compound with him. She came about two months after they arrived—and she was there eight months. Her name was Valentina Sanchez." He slipped his phone from his pocket and swiped it a few times. "A friend in the DEA sent me the drawing the sketch artist created based on their description of Valentina." He passed the phone across the table.

Grace forced herself to look at it.

The nose was a little off, but the eyes. Those were her eyes, her mouth, her hair—even her cheekbones. Grace might as well have taken a punch to the belly. She'd been hoping for a better answer—one that painted her in an honorable light. Something she could share with Hollis that wouldn't confirm his or Cord's theories—or her own. "I was his mistress—whether I was his assassin or not—this holds true. Whether I flipped or not… I was in a romantic relationship with an evil monster."

"That doesn't make you one," Blair said. "I was once married to an evil monster—Hector's brother. I got out. And it seems you did too."

"Did you do evil things while you were married to him? Did you know who he was?" Grace swallowed the lump in her throat.

Blair bit her bottom lip and tossed Holt another glance. "No. I didn't."

"Well, I did. I know I did. I can feel it. So, what does that make me?" She needed air. To get out of there. She stood. "Thank you for your time."

"Grace, are you going to see Hector?" Blair asked.

Grace inhaled deeply. "I don't know. He holds answers. I need some. And it's not like he doesn't know I'm alive and is already coming for me."

What did she have to lose?

# SIX

"Now that I think about it, she didn't actually say she was going to meet you, Hollis. Just that she had to leave at ten." Tish wrung a dish towel through her hands; worry etched around her mouth.

Hollis was fit to be tied. "She let you assume, though. She didn't set you straight."

Tish bit the corner of her bottom lip. "Well, no."

He'd taken a break from sandbagging and swung by to take Grace to an early lunch if she was available—if not, he'd eat a sandwich at the inn. But Grace had disappeared—voluntarily. What was she thinking? She hadn't even answered any of his texts or phone calls. Did she not realize how worried he would be given the circumstances?

Hollis pulled his phone from his pocket. Time to call Cord. He needed reinforcements to find her.

The door opened. Grace walked in and froze.

Yeah, busted. "Where have you been? I'm thinking you weren't teasing about not understanding common sense. Or do you now have short-term memory loss too? Or both? Which is it?" Fear had morphed into fury now that he knew she was unharmed. "Because you couldn't possibly be crazy enough to go off gallivanting around town when multiple people want to see you six feet under!" he bellowed, his temper getting the better of him.

"Hollis," Tish quietly warned.

"I mean that is just asinine." He all but shook the walls with his raised voice. His brain signaled him to calm himself. To stop carrying on. But his heart had been frayed and frazzled. "You could have been kidnapped, beat up—again—or worse, murdered and left for dead. Do you think I want to find your body for a second time? Do you have any clue what that would do to me? Do you even care?"

Grace straightened her shoulders and lifted her chin. He knew that look all too well. He'd crossed a line, set her off. She came at him with predatory eyes, and with more force than he realized she had, rammed his chest knocking his bulky frame back a step. Grace Thackery knew where to aim. "You. Don't. Own. Me." She shoved him again, but this time he was ready for her and blocked her. But she came at him again, wildness in her eyes. "If I want to leave this place and go to China, then I will." She went into fighting stance. "And if you *ever* raise your voice to me again, you will regret it."

It was almost like she didn't even see Hollis. As if she were speaking to someone in her past. But she was in fighting stance and unpredictable. He wasn't sure if he should get up in her face and physically end this… or run for the hills.

"Tish, leave this kitchen right now," Grace commanded with an authority and bite that sent a shudder through Hollis. This must be the Mad Max Peter and Crewcut had referred to.

Tish cleared her throat, but obeyed.

When Tish exited the kitchen, Grace got all up in

Hollis's grill. "Apologize," she demanded, fire and ice swirling in her shadowy eyes.

His temper flared again but those words of scripture blanketed his heart once more and cooled his ire.

*A soft answer turneth away wrath.*

Grace's fury was bottled deep from her past and her display was misguided, popping up now that she was being stressed—now that memories were flashing.

He lowered his voice, lightened his tone. "For what?" He held his hands up in surrender—showing her he was a safe place. Maybe in her rocky past, her only place to fall was on thorns. He'd seen some of her scars. But Hollis would never be one to rip or shred Grace. "For trying to protect you? For worrying about your safety? For freaking out?"

Like reaching for a cornered animal, he kept his eyes locked on hers and eased his outstretched hands to her face, cradling her cheeks. "It's me, Grace. I'm not your enemy. Not ever."

She stared at him, then blinked and the light of the Grace he knew popped back into her gorgeous ebony eyes. "I don't know what came over me. You yelled at me…"

"I am sorry for that, Grace." He made a mistake. "What triggered this behavior?" Was it her secretive venture? Had she discovered new information or recovered new memories?

She spun and sank into a kitchen chair. "I don't know. It's as if I'm outraged over something—and it bursts through uncontrollably. Takes over everything. I can't explain it. It scares me."

Scared him too. If it got so out of hand he couldn't talk her down… He'd have to use force or she could hurt him—probably not severely, but give him a serious run for his money. *May it never come to that.* Grace's prowess and power unnerved him; and he admired her fiercely too. Her strength didn't intimidate him. "Where were you? What was so important that you'd risk your safety and my sanity?"

His phone rang. "Kali from the café," he said and answered. "Hey, Kali."

"Hollis, I'm sorry to bother you but my car is stalled out on Muddy River Road. It's flooded. Can you tow me out? I tried calling Trevor at the towing service, but they're backed up and he's out on a call. I totally have to get to work."

This was going to be happening more often if this rain didn't halt ASAP. "On our way." He filled Grace in as they hopped in the truck. "Now isn't the time, we have to deal with Kali, but our earlier conversation isn't over, Grace."

"Which one? I may have short-term memory loss, now too." She arched an eyebrow, but he spotted the measure of playfulness in it.

"I am sorry for how I said what I said. I'm not sorry for what I said."

"Say that again."

When he glanced over, she was grinning. "You know what I mean, Grace. I was terrified. I don't want to lose you. Don't want someone to hurt you. I believe you can take care of yourself one hundred percent. But you don't have any memory which makes your predicament more dangerous."

"I know."

They pulled to the shoulder. Three feet ahead, the middle of the road was submerged in water. "Guess she thought she could make it."

"Guessed wrong," Grace muttered and hopped out of the truck. Hollis grabbed the chains and trudged over.

Kali poked her head out the window. "I thought I had it. Sorry!"

"When in doubt, back out." Hollis sighed and went to work securing the chains from her car to his truck. Kali hopped in the back seat of his truck.

He pulled her vehicle from the waters. "Let's get the car to Trevor's then we can drop you at work."

"I owe you both free coffees," Kali said.

"I won't forget that," Grace said and Kali snickered. "Do you have a ride home after your shift?"

"Yeah, my mom can pick me up. Hopefully, I can drive my car by then."

He drove straight to Trevor's and dropped off Kali's car. They made small talk on their way to the Muddy Brewhaha. "River is rising so expect more flooded streets and be careful," Hollis said as he pulled to the front door.

"Will do." She waved and ran inside.

"All in a day's work," Hollis muttered. "So…"

"I need to get to Tish's."

Hollis grimaced but kept his cool. No point arguing. Tish's inn was just off Main Street and not far from the Brewhaha. He parked behind Grace's car. "What was so important, Grace? Please talk to me."

Not for leads or to have some sense of control. To be a support for her. The more she kept from him, the greater the chasm that developed between them and quite frankly, he hated the distance, but it might be for the best.

His heart was getting too tangled up and his head fuzzy. Lines that should be straight and clear were blurring.

She reached for the door handle and paused, but then

opened the door and hopped out into the rain. "Gotta grab my other pair of rain boots if we plan to sandbag again later," she said and approached her car. The wind picked up and Hollis caught a whiff of something familiar.

Like tar.

Where had he smelled that before?

No!

He sprang from his truck and was already sprinting for her. "Grace, don't unlock—"

She clicked her fob.

*Beep-beep.*

He dove on top of her.

*Boom!*

Her car exploded into flames and smoke billowed into heavy pillars. Ringing pierced his ears and a rush of heat enveloped them, the impact blowing them several feet away. Car alarms were set off all along the street.

Police sirens squawked.

Hollis shielded Grace as debris fell with the rain, littering them and the surrounding area. The smell of iron, smoke and burning metal smacked his senses and produced a metallic taste on his tongue. "Grace, you okay?"

Her face was smudged with soot and mud, her hair covered in bits of ash. She only nodded. The bomb must have accidentally delayed. Otherwise, she'd have been toast. He thanked God and laid his forehead on hers. "I need to know where you went, Grace."

Someone was not playing around. It was possible by now the bad guys knew she had amnesia making her useless to them, and were simply ending her to tie up loose threads. But who were the bad guys?

He helped her to her feet and steadied them both.

Cord strode over. The fire department had already worked to put out the fire—the rain not enough to do the trick. First responders met them with a dozen questions and prompts to go to the hospital. Both Grace and Hollis declined.

His head split in two from the impact and every voice and noise sounded like it was underwater, but that would last only a day, maybe two. He coughed and put his arm around Grace who was also hacking but trying not to make a big deal out of it.

"Get cleaned up and let's talk," Cord said. "It's not only Grace's life at stake. That could have taken out the whole street."

Grace rubbed her temples. "No, it couldn't have. It was concentrated to the radius of the car and went straight up."

Hollis stared, stunned. He needed to get used to this Grace—the one who knew things like radiuses of bomb explosions. "She's right."

Grace's eyes went wide. "Where's Tish?" She bolted across the street, weaving between onlookers, guests at the inn, news crews who'd already arrived and firefighters.

"Grace!" Hollis took off after her. When he reached the kitchen, Tish was inside at the table crying, Grace soothing her.

"Tish, how you faring?"

"Shaken up is all. Worried about you and Grace."

Grace hugged her tightly and sniffed, coughed. "I'm so sorry. This is all my fault."

"It's no one's fault but whoever set that bomb on your car," Tish said and scowled.

"Did you see anyone suspicious outside today? Since Grace returned from her mystery adventure?" Hollis met Grace's glare with a withering look of his own. Seems like someone might have followed her and not liked where she went or what happened when she got there, then set the bomb once she returned—when she and Hollis were arguing or when they left to help Kali.

"I haven't noticed anyone around who shouldn't be. Cord has driven by regularly. Deputy Jordan has driven by and walked the property every hour. Guests who belong here." Tish wrapped her hands around a dainty cup of tea. "Grace, don't blame yourself."

Grace kissed Tish's head. "No one to blame but me."

"Not true." She sighed. "I put some of your clothes from the dryer in Room C."

Hollis would have to get some from his truck. He followed Grace into the dining area. "When we get cleaned up, after we talk to Cord, you and I are having a conversation."

Grace worked her jaw and met his stare. "Okay. Okay, Hollis, you win. But you won't like it. I certainly don't."

How bad could it be?

Hollis glanced out the window. Explosive. It could be explosive.

Grace sat on the edge of the bed. She'd cleaned up and dressed twenty minutes ago, but she struggled to leave the room. To face Hollis and probably Cord. She rubbed her cheek—tender from the scrape of the sidewalk when she landed. She'd taken three naproxen. Her ears still hummed and sounded muffled. Based on all the scars she possessed and the former broken bones, she chalked this up to child's play. Nothing broken. Nothing lacerated. A blessing to be sure.

Well, time to take some more medicine, swallow the

pill as she told Hollis the truth about her past. What she'd probably done. Grace worked hard to be brave, courageous. To channel that warrior—even if she'd been fighting for the wrong team—who lived dormant inside her. But right now, she was just Grace Thackery. SAR volunteer, employee of the Muddy River Inn, friend, neighbor and terrified lonely woman. Lurking beyond these walls were cold-blooded killers and they wanted her dead if she couldn't produce Dr. Sayer—someone wanted her dead regardless.

She needed to find that woman. It had been over two years. What was she doing to survive, to stay off the grid? A gentle knock came.

"Grace?" Hollis asked. "You aren't asleep, are you? In a coma?" The teasing banter was back. She adored the playful Hollis. Loved that he didn't give her pitiful looks like some of the Cottonwood locals. He'd pushed her to move forward with this new normal—her new life—in many ways.

She'd been wrong to charge him earlier. It had all happened so fast.

He'd pushed her—no, demanded answers—treating her as a child. And that was it. A switch had flipped.

But he didn't understand her humiliation, guilt or shame. How could he? He'd no doubt been a good son, a great brother, a soldier, and now a man who dedicated his life to helping search for and rescue people. How could he possibly comprehend the darkness that seemed to lurk inside Grace—that boiling rage waiting to flare up at any moment?

She could have hurt him earlier. But then his compassion and tender words brought a psalm to her heart that she'd memorized only recently, giving her the inner strength to hold back. To be still. She had imagined lying in green pastures by quiet waters.

And it had worked. Truth had fought the anger, and it had won.

Today.

"Grace?"

"Coming." She'd almost forgotten Hollis was at her door. She opened it, and he stepped inside.

"Thought we'd have more privacy up here."

"Where's Cord?"

Hollis eased into the wingback chair by the fireplace. He leaned forward, his elbows on his knees. His fingers locked together and rested under his chin. "I told him we needed to talk first and if what you tell me is pertinent to your case, we would fill him in. As far as the logistics of what happened, I already gave a statement. But you'll have to give yours."

"Protocol."

"Yes." He waited. Watched.

Her stomach spasmed. Blood whooshed in her ears, her heart beat against her chest. She swallowed. "I had a memory…" When she finished telling him about Hector Salvador, meeting Holt and Blair McKnight and their grave news, she dropped onto the edge of the loveseat adjacent to Hollis, but refused to look him in the eye for fear of what she might see—what she *would* see. Disgust. Disappointment. For the first time, possibly even pity.

"You want to go see him, don't you?" Hollis asked.

"Yes. He's my only link…even if it is a nefarious one." *Nefarious.* That word she could recall. Who her parents were? Nada. "You don't seem surprised."

Hollis stood and raked a hand through his hair.

"Have I ever invaded your privacy? Acted like I didn't trust you?"

Where was this headed? "No."

"And I wouldn't. But…" He kneeled in front of her, placed his hands on her knees. Tiny flecks of amber dotted his espresso irises. Torment was mixed in there too.

"But what?"

"Please don't hate me. Don't drop-kick me or anything."

Now wasn't the time to lighten the mood…only he wasn't attempting that. He was serious. "I could never hate you, Hollis. If anyone should hate someone it's you hating me."

He framed her face. "Never," he whispered. "I need you to know that we are in dire straits and I'm desperate to stop whoever is trying to kill you. So…after you left the computer, I checked the browser history."

She frowned. That must have been gone with other memories. "No joking, I don't recall anything about browser histories."

"I can see where you went on the internet. I know you searched for Hector Salvador. I researched him. Saw the articles. Know how dangerous he is. I've been unsure why you were searching him. I'm sorry."

Grace wasn't angry with him. She probably would have done the same thing if the roles were reversed. "I understand." Hollis would never check up on her simply out of paranoia or some possessive need to control her. He was at his wits' end. Join the club.

He eased onto the sofa with her, his thigh touching hers. "If you want to see him, I'll go with you. I won't go in, if you don't want me to. I trust you, Grace. With my life. I know you'll tell me important information."

This man. She'd just revealed she had been Hector's

mistress for at least eight months. A drug lord! A murderer. Gunrunner. Who knew what else he was responsible for? And he was trying to make sure she could trust him with her privacy.

"I don't deserve a friend like you, Hollis."

He laced his hand in hers, then brought it to his lips and kissed her knuckles. "I'll call the prison, find out when we can go. If we can."

"Can I be alone awhile?" she asked.

"Yeah."

"And then…then later would you mind bunking on the love seat in here? I don't want to be alone when night comes." So what? She was admitting to fear.

He tucked a strand of hair behind her ear. "I would do anything for you, Grace. I'm not afraid of your past. Don't you be." He shut her door with a quiet click and she curled up in a ball and wept until she was almost asleep. As she drifted off another memory forced its way into the forefront of her mind. So real. So vivid.

Grace stood over two graves. Dressed in a black dress. Eyes red and swollen. Heart shattered into a million pieces. She felt every single stab. She was younger. Much younger—in her teens. Hair a little shorter.

A man approached her. Only a little taller than her. He had thinning brown hair, a pointed nose and skinny lips. He wore dark-rimmed glasses that accentuated his ice-blue eyes. The rims were as red as hers. He put his arm around her and squeezed.

She felt admiration and fatherly love for this man. Was it her father? No.

"It's just the two of us, kid. They loved you more than anything."

"I know," she said. "What will I do now?"

The man led her away from the fresh graves. Grace

turned back. No names came. But she knew those graves had belonged to her parents. At some point in her late teens she'd lost them. She was orphaned. No family. If her memories returned, she'd still be alone.

At the edge of the road, he paused and retrieved a black box from his pocket. "I found this in your father's things. I suppose he meant to give it to you on your birthday in a few weeks. Your eighteenth…" They continued a conversation that felt blurred, fuzzy. Muffled.

Grace opened the box.

The locket! Her locket that she wore now. Given to her by her father. But he'd apparently died before then. He and her mother.

Grace looked up at the man wearing glasses and fell into his arms weeping.

When she opened her eyes, she wondered if she had dreamed it. No, it had been a memory.

Where was that man now? Who was he? An uncle? A family friend perhaps. He might be searching for her. They'd estimated her age to be late twenties to early thirties. This memory must have happened ten to fifteen years ago—if they estimated her age correctly. Surely, this man was looking for her.

Grace touched the locket, tried to open it. As usual, it was hopeless. It might be time to have it pried open, even if it did ruin it. Time to see if photos were inside and would force a memory.

She went into the bathroom and washed her face, looked at her reflection in the mirror. Before long, she would be seeing Hector Salvador face-to-face. Talking to him might bring a memory. There were some concerning him she didn't want to ever remember.

She splashed more cold water on her cheeks as another memory surfaced.

Grace stood in a luxurious spa bathroom, washing her face. A woman knocked on the door frame with a cheery smile, bright blue eyes and hair so blond it was almost white. Cut short at her chin. "Be careful, Max. If Hector finds out...he'll try to kill you."

Grace grinned, cocky and sure of herself.

"Don't you worry about me."

"Well, I do," she said and fluffed her hair. "That's what best friends are for. Worry about one another and watch each other's back."

Then the memory was gone.

There had been a best friend. One who worried and warned her. Watched her back. Like Hollis.

"Grace?" he called as if on cue. "Can I come in?"

She entered the bedroom. "Of course."

He held a blanket and pillow. Dressed in sweatpants and a T-shirt. Going to sleep on a cramped love seat for her. To keep her safe in the night.

"Thank you," she said.

He plopped his pillow on the end of the love seat and spread out his blanket. "I've slept in worse places."

"I probably have too."

The room grew silent. She hadn't meant at the compound, but there it was. In the air between them. Her past.

"I'll stay awake until you sleep," he murmured.

She slid into her covers and pulled them up to her chin. This man was entirely too good for her. Memories or not.

When she opened her eyes, sunlight worked hard to stream through the dappled sky. The room was dim, only slivers of sunshine. Hollis sat on the love seat drinking a cup of coffee. What time was it? She checked her cell phone. Almost nine. She'd slept way past her normal time.

"I wondered if I should wake you. Concussion. Coma." He winked. The wall of tension that had been built last night was gone.

She giggled. "I guess I was exhausted."

"I guess. Feeling reenergized?"

She nodded.

"Good. We're seeing Hector Salvador today."

# SEVEN

Grace hadn't been sure what to expect. A hardened criminal. Dead eyes. Maybe even prison tattoos like she'd seen on that one show. She hadn't expected this.

Hector Salvador sat comfortably in a plastic chair, pulling off an orange jumpsuit. How was that possible? While he was an evil man, he was striking. Charcoal-colored luxurious hair, cut short but not enough to do away with some natural curl. No hints of gray for a man in his late forties. He'd made sure to keep fit in prison.

Grace swallowed and slowly approached him. Alone. Hollis had remained outside per her request. In this room, prisoners had open access to guests. Unchained. Armed guards stood in every nook and cranny.

Her eyes met his. Black as night canopied by even darker lashes. For a brief moment, she caught his surprise at seeing her.

She reached the table and he stood, graciously gesturing for her to have a seat. Might as well be entertaining a guest in his home. Guess he kind of was. "Valentina," he said in heavy Hispanic accent. "Have you been missing me?"

Grace eased into a chair, every nerve jumping.

"I suppose you know by now that I don't know where Dr. Sayer is."

A thick eyebrow rose. "You come to visit and offer no pleasantries?" He *tsked* her and smirked. "You can do better than that."

Was he toying with her? "All right. How've you been, Hector? Me? I've been roughed up, left for dead and stuck with amnesia for the past two years."

The man had hiding his emotions down to a fine art. Not even a tick of his cheek. "Is that so?"

"Yes. Imagine my surprise when two of your men tried to drown me in a ditch if I didn't give them the location of the doctor." She told him how she'd connected the dots that led her here.

Hector rubbed his chin. "Let's say I believe you. What do you want? You think I sent men to kill you? You have proof that they work for me? Many Hispanic men in the world, Valentina."

"Seems odd, though, doesn't it? That two men show up wanting the doctor…a doctor who worked many years in Bogota, where you happened to live and own a lab where that doctor worked on the side. Please, stop playing games. I need to figure out who I am. And you, Hector—you're the only tangible link to my identity."

He tipped his head to the side and seemed to consider her plea. What did he know? Would he tell her?

"We met in a nightclub at a resort in Belize. You were exquisite in that red dress. Caught my eye immediately." He seemed angry at that memory. "It was a whirlwind affair."

Her stomach knotted.

"You came to my home. You lived with me."

"And?"

"You want details?"

She worked to not curl her lip. "I want details about me. What did I tell you? Where did I say I came from?"

"Why? None of it was true. I checked." Hector sighed. "Not even your name. All lies."

Same thing Peter Rainey said. It had all been lies. But what exactly?

"Did I betray you?" She licked her bottom lip. This man had the power to kill her, to blow up her car—if it had been under his orders to do so. He wasn't the only one trying to murder her.

Hector leaned forward and she flinched. His expression turned amused. "Maybe you do suffer memory loss."

"I am telling you the truth now. If I had my memories, don't you think I'd have handled your men myself? Not come here to get you to admit to trying to kill me. It doesn't matter. You're in prison either way."

"You did not betray me because what we had was never real. I blame myself for falling into the trap." He shrugged. "But I did have a very good time."

She ignored his statement. He was trying to get under her skin and it was working. "So, I never flipped on you and went into witness protection?"

He laughed. "Valentina, please." He waved her question off as if it were preposterous.

"Then who am I? And if I lied to you, how do you know I'm not in WITSEC?"

"I don't. For certain. But this I do know. When I left for the States to aid my sister-in-law, I left you behind at the estate. One day later, DEA showed up, but before you and Patsy could be taken into their custody—before they could infiltrate the lab—it went up in a blaze and you and she disappeared. Like wind. I didn't even know you'd escaped until loyal men of mine confessed you and she were gone."

What did this mean? That she had some inside information that the DEA were coming and she needed to run? "What were you making in that lab? Why was she helping you? Why would I escape with her? If I even did."

He reached across the table and stroked her hand. She pulled it away. "I think, Valentina, the better question is why did you happen to be at that nightclub—that resort—when I was? How did you know the kinds of things I'd like—including women in red? Why did you agree to come and live with me? How did you escape before the DEA even saw your face, and flee the country with the doctor? And better yet, why would you run from Bogota to little ole Mississippi? Not even a big city. But a small town. These men after you…they have yet to find the doctor after two whole years. Who would look in Mississippi? And even when they did—there was no clue."

Grace's heart beat wildly.

"You know what I discovered about you, after you left and I realized you were not who you said you were?"

"What?" she whispered.

"Nothing." He leaned in. "I even had things you touched searched for fingerprints and a hairbrush sent to a private lab—for a price. Valentina…you do not exist in this world. How can that be?" He cocked his head, studied her face. "Even if you were a federal agent of any kind, that extensive DNA testing would give answers to me."

Grace didn't exist. Nothing at all, not even a birth record had popped when he got ahold of her DNA?

"Who can make that kind of thing happen?"

"Major criminals?" she almost choked saying it. Was she so vile that someone with hacking skills had erased her from everything?

"Possibly but unlikely. Why take the doctor?"

She wasn't sure that she had. Hector seemed to believe it, though. "I don't know."

"Valentina, you're a spy."

The words overwhelmed her. "Like James Bond?"

He splayed his hands. "I suspect. You're not DEA or you wouldn't have set my lab on fire."

"Who says I did?"

"I have eyes, Valentina, in all places and at all times."

"Not enough to see me run or where I tucked the doctor, if I tucked her anywhere," she muttered.

Hector relaxed in his chair. "I always liked that spicy tongue. You torched my lab. You didn't want the DEA to find the research there."

"The toxin they were working on?"

He shrugged. He'd be stupid to admit that was what he was making even though the scientists taken into custody testified to it—at least they speculated.

If what he was saying was true, then it was possible she'd been sent to recover that toxin and all its research so he couldn't use it. It must have been deadlier than just able to harm some poppy crops.

"I see you're connecting dots."

"What was that toxin going to do?"

"Everything I do makes me rich, Valentina. Even inside these walls, I am rich and powerful."

"Call off your men. I don't know where the doctor is."

"I have no idea what you are talking about." His smirk disagreed. "But if I did—hypothetically—I might be willing to tighten their leash, but not when it comes to finding Dr. Sayer. She did not leave without some of that research, I assure you. And while I may be in here, I still continue to have control over my empire, which means I'd still want that particular toxin. Hypothetically, of course."

"To ruin crops?"

"For what I want? Yes. Again—hypothetically—it could be much more dangerous. Deadly. It would be worth sending in a CIA agent who is cunning and smart and able to handle herself with a man like myself to retrieve it. Who knows? Maybe you have it, Valentina. Not Dr. Sayer. Maybe you killed her so she couldn't recreate it." His smile sent a chill along her spine. "I imagine you've killed often, James Bond."

That was it. She'd heard enough. "If I find out you're lying—"

"You'll what? Kill me too? Careful who you threaten, *mujer hermosa*."

Grace stood and walked away.

"No kiss goodbye?"

She exited to the sound of Hector's laughter.

If Hector was right, Grace was on the right team. A good guy who had done terrible things—immoral and corrupt things—to infiltrate monstrous people. To protect the citizens of America—the world? The idea ought to make her feel better, but it didn't. Not at all.

Grace probably wasn't a person of faith before her accident. Would she have ever chosen a faith-filled life if she hadn't taken a fall and lost her memories? If her slate hadn't been wiped clean?

She had no idea but at the moment, her blank mind felt more like a blessing than a downfall. *Lord, I trust You to make something good of this. I suppose You already have. I'm scared I might slip into old ways if my*

*memories return—I've been doing some bad things now.
I'm afraid I won't be able to handle all the things I've
done, the people I've hurt. And where is all this rage
and anger coming from? What could I possibly be so
mad about? Please show me what to do.*

Hollis rose from a gray bench, worry in his eyes.
"Well? Anything useful?" He pulled her to his chest
and held tight. "How are you holding up?"

Grace wrapped her arms around his strong back and
clung to him, letting all his strength seep into her. She
was mentally, emotionally and physically exhausted.
From the confusion, running for her life, being repeat-
edly attacked and living in day-to-day uncertainty.
"Let's get out of here and we'll talk."

She needed to get out of this prison—and the one
that held her life hostage.

Hollis remained silent as he escorted Grace to his
truck. Her conversation with Hector had rattled her further. More than anything, Hollis wanted to make this
debacle go away, wanted to help rescue her memories
so she could sort out her life and move forward.

Except that moving on might be away from Cottonwood and Hollis.

He'd be losing his best friend.

Grace was who he called first when he heard something funny, when he was in a rotten mood and needed
his spirits lifted, the first person he wanted to share
good news with and even bad news, like when his sister, Greer, had been hunted by a killer. Who would he
share these things with if she left?

Maybe she wouldn't leave to return to a life of
crime—no way—but when her memories surfaced,
she might want a bigger life. In a bigger place.

Just like Mary Beth.

Grace might want to leave to "find herself" too. Where would that leave Hollis?

Alone.

And if he were honest, heartbroken. He'd tried to keep his heart fortified, to keep Grace from burrowing into it, lodging there. Hollis had done a pitiful job. Because that's what she'd done—made a home there. He wasn't sure what to do with that.

Right now, nothing. The only thing he knew to do to protect himself was to get some distance, but that was impossible. Grace needed him. He needed to keep her safe.

Once they were inside the truck and moving onto the interstate, Grace shared her conversation with Hector. Hollis listened quietly, filing away the information and trying to discern if this drug lord was sending her down a wild trail. After Grace finished, Hollis agreed that Hector's theory of Grace being CIA seemed more plausible than anything else when all the tedious facts were considered, especially about the DNA. They'd run fingerprints and nothing had popped. But if her fingerprints were never in the system for anything, including a background check, then there would be no reason for Grace to appear. But the lengths that Hector had gone to...something should have turned up if only minuscule.

"Help me make some sense of this, Hollis. If I'm a CIA agent, then why haven't they found me? Been able to track me?" She laid her head against the seat and groaned. "All I know about spy stuff is what I've seen watching movies and TV with you."

"If they think you died, they'd wipe you out of the system. Not that you'd have been in a system to be found anyway. The kind of agent you might have been would be top secret." What he didn't tell her was if the CIA was responsible for leaving her for dead then that could be a reason they hadn't descended and why no information—not even false cover information—existed on her. She'd been burned. But why would the CIA want her eliminated?

Peter Rainey must have been CIA too. The way he stole cars, extracted rental information and then said he'd betrayed her. Before he could reveal any truth, he'd been assassinated and not likely by Hector's men. Maybe the good guys weren't as good as they should be.

Grace picked at her nails. "Let's say I am a spy. I was undercover to get intel. Then I got it. Burned the place after taking the research and toxin so the DEA or bad guys wouldn't get it and I left with Dr. Sayer. What happened between leaving Colombia and making it to Mississippi? If I was bringing her to a safe house, who intervened? Followed me? Tried to kill me? And where is that research or toxin—or both? And where is Dr. Sayer now?"

"Truth?" He glanced over to see her wheels turning. "I don't think Hector's men would have followed you from Colombia. Hector said he didn't even know you were gone at first—until one of the men discovered it. And he was in a mess of his own here in the States and unable to give commands. So, that means—"

"Whoever tried to kill me in the shed—most likely who killed Peter—was an agent and Peter probably was too. Dirty agents? Or…was I?" Grace's lip trembled. "Even if I was on the winning team, I did terrible things, Hollis. I don't know if I can forgive myself for that."

Hollis understood guilt. Even in war, on covert missions, people died and while it was part of it—part of fighting evil men—it always took a toll. Those men haunted him at times, especially at night when he was alone with his thoughts. In the quiet. Grace would have to deal with her past, but now she had a way to do that—the same way as Hollis. God. Even when it felt like Hollis was alone, he never truly was, and neither was Grace.

"Let's deal with that when we know the truth. Don't feel guilty over something you aren't even certain about."

"I am certain I had a relationship with a drug lord and murderer."

She'd probably been undercover and yes, compromised her morals—if she even had any prior to the amnesia. "Grace, you are not the same person. I've said it once and I'll keep saying it until you believe it. You can't change the past, not the circumstances or your choices. All you can do is make better decisions and live honestly now. I mean, think about it. God knew all you did in Colombia and before that. And yet, He still rescued your heart when you walked down that aisle and cried out for Him to be your Lord and Savior. He saved you, Grace. By grace. You didn't know what you'd done—but He did. And He loved you anyway."

Grace's eyes filled with tears and she bit her bottom lip.

"He doesn't want you or me or anyone wallowing in our messed up past. Ask for forgiveness, change your ways and live a life that honors Him. That's how I manage. I've done things that condemn me too."

"I guess I feel like I don't deserve any of it."

Hollis chuckled but only because he understood so well that feeling. "Honey, none of us deserve that kind of love, mercy or grace. That's why it's a gift. Open it up like a Christmas present and enjoy it." He clasped her hand, and she squeezed his.

"You're a good, good man, Hollis. A godly man. I admire you so much."

"We got about an hour before we get home. You go right ahead and keep up the sweet talk. I like it." He winked and she laughed. A real laugh. Exactly what he wanted to see lighting up her face. No more guilt. No more heavy talk. At least for an hour.

But those words wiggled into his heart and warmed it.

They listened to the radio, went to a drive-thru and purchased coffees and muffins, then pulled in at the SAR facility. Hollis was cautious and swept the place, making sure it was secure. A couple of volunteers were doing some training with the dive equipment.

Grace followed Hollis into his office and plopped on the small leather sofa against the wall. Hollis chose his office chair. "What do you wanna do, Grace?"

"I want to find Dr. Sayer."

"Me too. If you did hide her and she's remained there for this long, you hid her well. Remind me not to ever play hide-and-seek with you."

She rubbed her locket and grabbed one of the throw pillows he used to nap on. "Can you call Wilder at CCM? See if his analyst can do some deep, dark digging. I know if I'm a CIA agent, it's practically impossible but on the off chance...?"

Hollis nodded and made the call to Wilder. He answered on the second ring.

"Hollis, any news?" he asked.

"Yeah, actually."

"Hold on." The sound of a door opening and closing filtered through the line, then heavy footsteps—like work boots on wood—then a knock. "I'm in the control room with Wheezer. Gonna put you on Speaker. Go ahead."

He gave him the rundown of the day and the information.

Hollis put Wilder on Speaker too.

Keys clicking against a keyboard came to life. "I'm going to do a search on Valentina Sanchez," Wheezer said. "Add keywords like your description, locations… Hector…" The clacking noise was faster than lightning.

"What's that on monitor six?" Wilder asked Wheezer.

How many monitors did this guy use?

"A pretty lady, but not Grace," Wheezer replied and continued clacking. "Hector clearly liked lovely women."

Grace's cheeks turned red.

"Nothing is hitting, guys. Sorry. I can go even deeper, see if I can snag an image of Hector with you and follow that, but if you worked for the CIA and they burned you—not even I can find you."

"Any other news on Dr. Sayer?" Hollis asked.

"I've been working to trace her in the past two years, but she's off the grid. Major off. Which means someone has helped her become a ghost or she's dead. We did find a bank account. She withdrew every single penny six months before she disappeared."

"Seems like she knew she was going to need money," Hollis said. Did Grace or someone else forewarn her? "How much was it?"

"A hundred and fifty grand. But two thousand dollars were regularly withdrawn each month for about two decades prior. The money went to a home in Atlanta for the physically challenged. Dr. Sayer had a younger sister with cerebral palsy. We called and found out that her sister's account was prepaid for five years, but she passed away about six months ago. No one claimed the body, or the money. It's in a private account that was set up by Patsy. She either has no idea her sister died because she's not making contact and there is no way of contacting her, or she knows but thought it too dangerous to reach out for the body, the money or anything—including a funeral. Peggy—her sister—was cremated."

"Or Patsy's dead. Dead people don't claim money." Grace hung her head and raked her hands through her hair. "But if she is alive and knows, that's horrible. I can't imagine not being able to say goodbye to the ones I loved for fear of getting killed in the process. But if they want the toxin, she wouldn't be killed."

"Not until they had what they wanted. She is surely smart enough to know once the toxin was finished, she would be expendable." Hollis rocked in his office chair. "The question is, was Patsy at the compound making this toxin of her own free will or was she forced into it?"

The room remained silent. Finally, Wheezer spoke. "We'll keep on it, Grace."

"Thank you," she said.

They said their goodbyes and hung up.

"Patsy is the key."

"I agree." A boom of thunder sent Grace a foot in the air. The woman was a scared rabbit, but fighting to be brave. Hollis crossed the room and sat beside her, slinging his arm around her. "How about we get some real food, and talk about what to do next?"

"I think the next thing we'll have to do is pull more cars out of flooded roads and ditches." The thumping of rain on the roof was a sure sign this town was in trouble if the system didn't pass through soon.

"You're right."

"I need to look at the radars and track the storm. If residents need to evacuate, I can't be sitting on my hands." Grace stood and stretched.

One of the volunteers poked his head in the office. "Hey, glad you're here. We've got an issue. Mulberry subdivision is in a flood zone and the yards are already under water. Satellite system shows heavy rain for the next three days."

"I'll call the sheriff. Thanks."

Felt like more than rain flooding his world lately. If they could only catch a break. As Hollis looked out the window at the rain coming down, an eerie feeling tightened his chest. If Grace was a spy, then they'd continue to send agents—agents trained to kill.

Hollis was prepared to go down swinging.

# EIGHT

Grace breezed through the kitchen and into the dining area with a tray of eggs sunny-side up, a plate of toast and bacon, two coffees and a bowl of fruit. She placed them in front of Dr. Jones and his wife. They always had breakfast on Thursday mornings at the inn, then Dr. Jones went to work and left Mrs. Jones lingering over a third cup of coffee and a paperback. They were like clockwork with their routines. Grace envied them that kind of familiarity. She wanted someone to settle into routines with—a place they always ate breakfast, a park they walked in every evening after dinner.

"Thank you, Grace," Dr. Jones said. "How are you feeling?" The entire town knew about the explosion—it had made the news. Cord had kept Grace from TV cameras, giving all the interviews. No one else needed to see her on camera and hunt her down. She had enough psychos after her already.

"Much better, thanks. Enjoy."

She carried her coffee pot to the table in the corner near the window and bookshelves. Hollis sat eating pancakes and bacon and studying something on his laptop. "Warm up your coffee?" she asked.

He looked up and smiled. "Always." Last night they'd

taken Cord up on his offer and stayed there again and would indefinitely. But during the day, Grace had to work. Wanted to keep some normalcy. And if they were to take off and flee, it would only send the bad guys chasing her. They'd all agreed to stay in Cottonwood. Keep to public places. And have someone around for added protection. At least if unfamiliar faces cropped up in town, they'd be on alert. In an unfamiliar city no one was recognizable and the risk spiked.

"As soon as breakfast is over, Tish says I'm free. It's soup or chili and corn bread on the dinner menu tonight and she can handle that solo."

Hollis nodded and sipped his coffee. "Good plan. We have to finish sandbagging and work on an evacuation plan if it gets worse. Cord said half of the Mulberry subdivision has cleared out. Water's up to the front stoops and porches. Some leaking in homes already."

"Where did they go?"

"Hotels, friends, family. Insurance will cover it if they have flood insurance, but it's still a headache."

Dr. Jones stood, catching Grace's attention. He slipped on his white doctor's coat and like a match being lit, a memory ignited.

A woman with the same dark hair, skin coloring and eyes as Grace's entered a large living room. She smiled and hung up a white doctor's coat.

"Hey, honey. You eaten anything yet?"

Grace—maybe sixteen or seventeen—was curled up on a white sofa with a bowl of cereal. "This count?"

Her mother grinned, but she looked tired around the eyes. "Is it bran or sugar galore?"

"Sugar galore, but it says it's fruity so…" She shoveled in another bite. "Dad gonna be home tonight?"

"He's still out of town. Be back Friday."

Grace glanced at the doctor's coat. Dr. Newark. Pathology.

The memory faded.

"Grace," Hollis snapped and Grace blinked. "Hey, I said your name three times. What's going on?"

"I got a memory. Of my mom. I look like her and her name—I have a name!—is Newark. She worked in pathology. But I don't know where or what her first name is. Or my name. Just that I liked cereal and my dad traveled for work."

Hollis beamed. "This is great news."

"It's possible my mom knew Dr. Sayer. We need to call CCM and have them try to find links between the two. Find a first name for my mom which might link to something that would tell me my name."

Hollis called CCM, giving them the new information. They promised to get right on it. He hung up and Grace sat across from him. "I don't know my mom's first name...or anything really but I know deep down— I feel it—we were close and I miss her."

"I miss my mom," Hollis said. "She was the best. Worked her fingers to the bone to make sure Greer and I had everything we needed after my father abandoned us. When I turned sixteen, I got a job and tried to give her my paycheck to help us out. I remember she cried and hugged me but said, 'Hollister Montgomery, as long as I'm breathing and able, I'm supporting this family. Be a kid a little longer, but I love you so much for it.'"

Grace's eyes burned.

Moisture formed in Hollis's eyes. "That Christmas I bought her favorite perfume. After Dad left and it ran out, she'd stopped wearing it. Too expensive. At least for her. She always bought us what we wanted first. White Diamonds. I bought her a bottle every year until she passed. When I was back home visiting Greer this past April, the place still smelled like it."

"I wish I remembered what my mom smelled like."

"I wish you did too. Maybe you will. You've been having more vivid memories than you ever have before. This could mean they're about to unleash on you."

A bittersweet hope. "I wish the good memories would return. The rest—they can stay locked in an abyss."

Hollis laughed as his cell phone rang. "It's CCM." He answered.

"Hey, Hollis, it's Wilder. You're on Speaker."

"You are too. Go ahead."

"We've got some solid information."

Excellent.

"We found a Dr. Newark in pathology at George Washington University Medical. Lucinda Newark. Just texted you a photo."

Hollis checked his texts. Showed it to Grace. "Is that her? Your mom? From your memory?"

Grace stared at the photo, stunned. "Yes," she whispered. "That's her."

"Okay, then here's what we know. Lucinda Martinez married Henry Newark. One daughter, Lucy Anna Maria Newark."

Grace couldn't hold in the tears. She had a name—after her mother. Hispanic descent. A dad. Hollis squeezed her hand.

"Henry Newark worked in Washington, DC, as a data analyst for an advertising company. They lived in a suburb about fifteen minutes away in Virginia—I have an address. Lucinda was the head of the pathology department and did some lecturing at the university. Get ready for this... She was born and raised in Natchez,

Mississippi. Went to college and taught at Mississippi State. Moved after she married Henry. No records on how they met or even a wedding announcement—possibly eloped. All her family is deceased. Haven't been able to find too much on Henry Newark, at least not yet," Wheezer said.

Grace—Lucy—had ties to Mississippi on her mother's side. "Did you search properties or anything in Mississippi in my name or my mom's? If I am an agent and kept a safe house that no one knew about, it might be nearby."

"I didn't find anything yet. But I'll keep trying," Wheezer said.

"Did you find any ties to my parents and Dr. Sayer?"

"Not a one. Doesn't mean there isn't though," Wheezer said. "I'll keep digging. I'm sending over an article. It's…it's about their deaths, Grace. Or Lucy. What do you want to be called?"

She'd had so many names. Lucy, Valentina, Max, now Grace. Who knew how many more aliases? But Grace was who she felt like in the present. "Grace is fine." And it reminded her how much grace she needed.

"I sent it to Hollis's email. They died in a plane crash. A little over ten years ago. The thing is, Grace, the flight plan had them heading to Bogota when it went down. That's why I want to dig a little more thoroughly."

Grace and Hollis stared at one another.

"Thanks, y'all," Hollis said. "We appreciate all your work."

"We'll keep on it. Call you when we have something." Wilder hung up. Hollis opened his email and the article.

Grace began reading. They'd been on a vacation in South America. Didn't say where. Could they have been flying to Bogota—to Dr. Sayer? Was it a coincidence? The plane crashed in the ocean. Bodies not recovered. Three deceased. Mr. and Mrs. Newark and the pilot.

"I have much more information than ever before but also more questions. If they died a little over ten years ago, and my birthday in the memory was a few weeks before my eighteenth birthday, then I'm probably twenty-eight."

"I would suspect so."

"If my parents knew Dr. Sayer, how weird is it that I ended up at Hector's compound while Patsy was working for him on-site? Would I have known her too? Was she a prisoner of his and that's why I went? Being there might have been professional and personal. It explains why I allegedly took her with me and ran."

Hollis rubbed his neck. "I don't know. But if your mom is from Natchez and worked in Starkville at the university, and you were found on the riverbank in Cottonwood, then you were either caught while traveling from Starkville to Natchez or the other way around since we're located almost in the middle but closer to Natchez."

But which was it?

"We don't have to wait for Wheezer. It's not a leap to guess you may have owned a house and/or property—not necessarily in your name or your family's name. You're smart enough to know how to hide something like a private safe house. A place you never told a living, breathing soul about."

This was so much information to digest, Grace's mind whirled and buzzed.

Hollis clicked his tongue against his teeth. "I say we take a trip to Starkville and flash Patsy Sayer's photo around, and your mom's. You never know. What else do we have to lose?"

Nothing.

"What about sandbags and strategies?" she asked.

"I'll call in some other volunteers. They can meet up with Cord."

While Hollis made phone calls, Grace finished up breakfast, then they hopped in Hollis's truck and headed for Starkville, Mississippi—the college town where her mother had once taught. Not quite three hours away. There might be at least one professor still around who remembered her, even though it was nearly thirty years ago.

It was almost lunchtime when they arrived. They pulled onto campus. College students bicycled and congregated on sidewalks.

They knocked on office doors, waiting for classes to end to slip inside rooms and show Grace's mom's picture to professors and teachers. Bust after bust. She taught there before Grace was ever born but surely there had to be someone left who knew her or of her.

The dean? Even if he did know Lucinda, that didn't mean he'd divulge any information. Grace had zero proof that she was her daughter. They finally found his office.

Inside they were met by a woman with salt-and-pepper hair and a no-nonsense demeanor. "Can I help you?"

They made introductions and Hollis explained they needed to see the dean about a former professor. They gave a few details, keeping personal information to themselves. "Would you happen to know her?"

She gave it a quick glance. "She doesn't look familiar and the dean's very busy," the secretary said.

"I understand, but he could be a big help to us, Ms...."

"Miss. Ryland. Judith."

"Judith. If he says no, then fine. But...please ask." With those eyes, Hollis was sure to get his way.

She sighed and hit the intercom button.

After waiting almost twenty minutes, the dean gave them his attention.

Tall with stark white hair and kind eyes, he greeted them with handshakes and invited them to sit across from his desk. Grace and Hollis revealed her situation— minus the murderous attempts, but a tragic accident that resulted in amnesia and that they were tracking relatives.

"I can't imagine your plight," he said. "I did know Lucinda. I came on three months before she left. She was a kind woman and her students doted on her. She was tough. To be honest, that's all I know, other than her departure felt abrupt—but she never offered any personal information. She only said she had another job and they expected her ASAP. Two weeks later, she was gone. I don't even know where."

And the plot thickened. Grace held in a frustrated sigh.

Hollis leaned forward. "Could you give us any personal information at all? Where she lived at the time? Colleagues who taught with her but are gone now?"

The dean nodded and got his secretary on the intercom. "Pull up the personal records on Lucinda Martinez, please."

About ten minutes later, the secretary buzzed him to check his emails. All records had been digitally scanned. Hallelujah!

"I can't forward these to you. They're confidential,

but it looks like she rented a small home about five minutes or so away from campus." He scrawled the address on a Post-it. "And it appears she was part of the college Christian Life ministry that helped students find church homes."

That made her mom a Christian, then. Surely, Grace must have known that faith early on as well.

Why had she strayed from it? Or ignored it?

"Other than that," the dean said, "I have nothing left to offer you."

They said their goodbyes and thanks, then entered the hall cluttered with students.

"If my mom rented a house here and lived in it until she moved and married my father, then she wouldn't have had any property to pass down to me. At least not in this area. Which means I wouldn't have any to have stashed Dr. Sayer in. At least nothing that I didn't purchase on my own."

Hollis weaved and bobbed through the throng of people, a backpack smacked into his shoulder and he grimaced. "Again, you're smart. You could easily have bought property under an alias—had someone you do know and trust purchase it for you. The possibilities are endless. Look at Peter Rainey and what he did with that rental car. No ID. What kind of car did he use before that rental? If he flew in, where would we find him on a flight manifest? You were trained. You'd know ways to stay off the grid."

"Like having a safe house in a college town or near here? Mississippi is an unlikely place to go."

"We may have to travel to Natchez where your mom grew up. Could be that whoever got the jump on you followed you from there but didn't catch up to you until after Sayer was hidden. Same could be said of Starkville though too. And it's smarter to stash someone here."

No one would seem out of place with it being a college town. People in and out all the time.

Hollis plopped on a bench outside a building. Grace perched next to him.

A woman knocked into a student.

"Miss Ryland! Watch where you're going!" he yelled and bent to pick up his spilled backpack. "Could you be any more extra?" he muttered to himself.

The dean's secretary stormed down the sidewalk, busting through the students like a whirlwind.

"Does that strike you as odd?" Grace asked. "You thinking what I'm thinking?"

"If you're thinking we should follow her," Hollis stood, "then yep."


Grace joined Hollis as he pursued the secretary to the lot. They were parked a few rows down. They waited until she backed out then got in the truck and kept a safe distance.

"You think she knows Dr. Sayer? Knew my mom?"

Hollis turned left about thirty seconds after Miss Ryland. "If she does or did, her acting skills are impeccable. And the Oscar goes to…"

"Who's Oscar?" Grace asked.

"Who's who? Oh…it's the most prestigious—top—award an actor can receive." He grinned. "How do you not know that? You got amnesia or somethin'?"

She chuckled and shrugged. "Maybe. I forget."

Miss Ryland led them into the middle of farmland. Nestled into the back half of the field on a small patch of property, a farmhouse came into view. Nothing but cornfields on one side of the house and cotton fields on the other. Hollis pulled to the shoulder of the road. He'd have to wait for the secretary to settle in. One dirt road. Two vehicles. She'd know she'd been followed.

"It's not a coincidence she busted out after we left and came here to the middle of nowhere—whether it's her home or not. When the crops are fully grown, the house will be almost impossible to see," Grace said.

"Seems like a smart place for a safe house, doesn't it?" Hollis asked. "Again, you are one smart cookie."

"If I even own this house." She bit her bottom lip.

"What's worrying you?"

"Just... How does one even become an agent?"

"Some people apply and go through training, but more covert agents...they're usually recruited."

"Why would I be recruited?"

Hollis eased onto the dirt road. By now, Miss Ryland had time to get inside. But not enough time to get Dr. Sayer out—if she was even in there. "Well, your parents died before you went to college and it appears you have no other family."

"Except that man at the funeral. It felt like I'd known him my whole life."

Hollis pulled the truck over. "We hoof it from here, okay? Don't want to give ourselves away."

"Like a navy SEAL mission?"

"Or a spy mission."

She gave him a sly grin. "I wonder if I had all my faculties—and do not make a joke—if I could take you, you big, bad navy SEAL."

Something about that idea sent a fire through his gut, shot clear into his neck and sent his pulse into dangerous levels. "I don't know—" his voice sounded dry and raspy even to himself "—but I'd be willing to give it my very best shot."

She leaned in, flirt in her eyes as she whispered, "I just hope your very best is good enough."

The truck felt like it'd heated up to a billion degrees and he swallowed hard. This was how she deceived men like Hector Salvador. Fiery charm with a heavy dose of flirt and confidence. And that thought brought him back to reality. They couldn't be sitting in a cornfield flirting with one another. A mission was only a few feet ahead. Not to mention they were friends, and he had to keep his heart in check.

"Let's put it to the test right now—on what's up ahead." He redirected them to the task on hand.

Grace stiffened and straightened her shoulders. "What's the game plan?" All business. Just like that.

"We give her the element of surprise, which means we aren't knocking and being polite."

"I have a feeling I'm good at not being polite. Sadly." She exited the truck and kept to Hollis's side as they stalked up the gravel drive, using the short cornstalks flanking it as cover.

Hollis crouched, sweeping the perimeter. A huge red barn was about twenty feet from the house. It was open and didn't appear to hold a vehicle other than a tractor. No garage. Looked like the only mode of transportation was the truck Miss Ryland had driven here in.

"Okay, I'm going in the back door. Stay here and if anyone runs, holler."

Grace nodded and Hollis's SEAL instincts kicked in. He moved with stealth staying low of windows until he was crouching at the back door. The sound of a TV came from inside. No other noise, but that didn't mean anything. Slowly, he opened the screen door, hoping it wouldn't squawk and screech. He carefully turned the door handle. Unlocked.

*Not smart, Miss Ryland.* Good thing he wasn't the bad guy. Cracking the door, he peeked inside a kitchen that hadn't been updated since the 1970s. Gold and green. Old faded linoleum. But the place was tidy and a hint of bacon still lingered in the air from breakfast.

He slipped inside. Voices came from the living room. He reached for his gun holstered to his ankle and walked straight into the living room.

"Ladies," he said and trained his gun on Dr. Sayer. He recognized her from the photos Wheezer had sent. "I'm not here to hurt anyone."

Miss Ryland rushed him, hollering, "Run, Patsy!"

Patsy flew out the front door. Hollis growled and subdued the secretary. "I'm a good guy, here."

Grace didn't holler for him. Had Patsy run the other way and Grace not seen her? Hollis wrenched Ryland's arm behind her back—without using too much force but enough to let her know he wasn't to be tested. "Dr. Sayer is in danger. We've come to help."

"Yeah, well, I don't believe you."

"You don't have a choice."

A truck door slammed. Patsy was going to get away. Moving quickly, Hollis surveyed the room, yanked the wooden blinds from the window and used the cords to tie Ryland's hands behind her, then he placed her in the chair by the window. "Stay."

Running out the front door he paused at the sight.

Grace stood in front of the truck, battery cables dangling from her hands.

"Going somewhere?" she asked Patsy, who'd hopped in the truck to run. She *tsked* her and stalked toward the driver's side. "Don't even think about pulling a weapon on me. You know what I'm capable of."

She must be banking on the fact that Patsy had no

clue she had amnesia. If Grace had gotten Patsy out of a foreign country from secret agents, then Patsy would know exactly what Grace was capable of, even if Grace had no inkling.

It worked.

Patsy's face blanched and she raised her hands in surrender. Grace tossed the cables—the woman had disabled the truck but she had no idea what an Oscar award was—and motioned with her index finger for Patsy to come to her. She didn't even have a weapon—while Hollis, at six-foot-three, had to tie up a petite secretary's wrists with a wooden blind cord.

Patsy slowly exited the truck. "Lucy! I thought you were dead—or—or I wasn't sure." She kept her distance. If this woman was a friend and Grace had stashed her for safekeeping, then why did she seem afraid of her? Something was off-kilter.

"I'm going to go inside and see about our Miss Ryland." He was fairly certain he'd scared her into sitting tight, but on the off chance she was braver than he anticipated and had gotten free, he better check. "I think you have things under control here."

"We'll join you." Grace thumbed toward Hollis. Patsy trudged along.

"Why did you wait so long to come for me?" Patsy asked.

"Inside, Doctor. Go." Grace's voice held serious authority, and a hint of the anger that popped out from time to time.

Inside, Miss Ryland worked extra hard to get out of the makeshift binds.

"If I untie these, will you behave?" Hollis asked.

"She will. It's okay, Judith," Patsy said. "Lucy, what

happened? Where have you been? You said you'd be back in a few days. A couple of weeks tops."

"Why didn't you leave then, when you realized I wasn't?" Grace asked.

"And go where? If Hector didn't find me, you can believe Clive would. I thought he found you. Killed you."

Clive. A new name to add to the mix.

Grace kept her face blank. "Well, he didn't."

"Have you been in hiding? Has it been too risky to come or contact me? Where's the toxin? The research? Is it safe? Out of Clive's hands?" Patsy's expression turned worried and she wrung her hands. "If that gets into the wrong hands, Lucy, you know what will happen."

Except she didn't.

"How have you stayed off anyone's radar?" Grace asked. "And how do you fit into this picture?" She pointed to Judith Ryland.

Judith licked her lips. "I knew your mom. I came to work in Administration two weeks before she moved, but she was kind and I liked her. I've helped Patsy stay underground all this time. A friend of your mom's is a friend of mine."

Patsy added, "Your mother and I had kept in touch. I knew she taught at State, so I did my own recon, found someone who knew her. Judith. Once I knew I could trust her, I confided in her."

Seemed like she used and manipulated her, but Judith must not see it that way. Hollis scowled, glanced between the two women. "So why run from Lucy?"

"It's been two years," Patsy said. "I had to be careful. I know what Clive meant to you, Lucy, and I was afraid he'd made his case all too well, which means you'd come for me—but not to protect me. To either kill me or trap me in a prison forced to research under Clive's direction—no thanks."

This Clive person must be powerful and diabolical.

"Then why not leave and go underground somewhere where Clive or I couldn't find you?" Grace asked.

"I don't play spy games, Lucy. I don't have farmhouses like this purchased under shell company names and fake passports, money from all nations. I don't have contacts all over the world to hide me or help me. So, I took my chances and stayed." She raked a hand through her hair. "Judith said you came in the office because you were trying to find a professor who happens to be your mother. So what game are you playing? We both know she's passed." She opened her mouth. And it was there in her eyes. "You got dosed with the toxin. You must have. Someone's after you and instead of showing up here—you went searching, hoping for information on your mother that might link to this house or me…"

Busted. Hollis didn't trust Patsy, but they had no other options. She was on to them. "Tell her, Grace."

"Is Grace the name you go by now? And who are you?" Patsy asked Hollis.

"I'm none of your concern."

"The truth is, Patsy," Grace said as she pinched the bridge of her nose, "I have no idea who I am." She told her every detail and everything that had transpired since Monday. "I don't even know who this Clive person is."

"Oh, child." Patsy jumped from her chair and embraced Grace. "You must have been dosed with the sample we had when we escaped Hector's compound. It affects your central nervous system and one of the many possible side effects is a coma and retrograde amnesia. You could have died if this man hadn't found you."

"She almost died anyway," Hollis said.

"I'll tell you everything, but we may not be safe here now. If Clive Epps is tracking you, you won't know—"

A bullet pierced the window and Judith Ryland fell to the floor dead.

"Down!" Hollis boomed and shielded Grace and Patsy. "We have to get out of here. Now!" They were going to take them all out!

The kitchen door busted in.

"There's a secret passage to the cellar," Patsy said as Hollis ushered them out of the living room and into the dining area. They took cover behind a large antique buffet. "But it's in the storage pantry in the kitchen under the rug. We can get into the cellar and climb outside."

Hollis put a finger to his lips, then motioned with two fingers his intent to sneak up on whoever had kicked in the door and disable him.

Grace shook her head like a dog with a bone.

He gave a resolute nod and slipped out from behind the buffet, tiptoeing to the door, gun in hand. Creaking on the stairs caught his ear, but noise in the living room did as well—the hall closet door squawked open. Two of them at least. Hector's men or agents? His thoughts were swirling a mile a minute.

Edging against the wall and creeping to the living room, he slipped behind the man built a lot like the assailant from the storage shed the other day. Using the butt of his gun, he knocked him unconscious, catching him before he thudded to the ground. He quietly dragged him into the hall closet and closed the door while Grace and Patsy hustled through the living room into the kitchen.

Hollis followed.

Suddenly he felt a presence behind him.

Grace moved like the speed of light and snatched

something, threw it. Hollis felt the air rush across his cheek in the wake of what she'd thrown.

The second assailant hissed and Hollis whipped around as the man's gun clattered to the floor. A kitchen knife protruded from his shoulder.

Hollis didn't have time to process Grace's quick move and perfect aim. He kicked the gun away, wrenched the man's wounded arm behind him, then quickly used a SEAL technique to press a pressure point and send the attacker night-night.

"Let's go!" Grace commanded and shoved Patsy toward the door; no need to use the secret passage now. Hollis was on their six. "He won't be out but maybe thirty seconds. Move. Move. Move."

Patsy tossed open the door and screamed as another dark-clad figure appeared.

Grace knocked her out of the way and in a few thrusts disarmed the attacker, kicked him in the face and slammed the door shut. "Other way! Go!"

Footfalls on hardwood coming from the living room put some pep in Hollis's step. They ran into the pantry and tossed aside the rug. Heart beating wildly, he shoved Patsy down, then Grace. He went last, working the rug over the secret door as he lowered it and entered the cellar.

Rotting vegetables smacked his senses. Dank. Patsy led them to a rickety ladder against the wall. Grace moved her aside and began climbing but Hollis stopped her.

"I'll go first." He didn't want any more surprises or Grace to end up with a bullet in her.

"No," she whispered.

"End of story." Hollis hauled himself up. "Send Patsy

after." He raised the cellar door an inch and peered out. Coast was clear. He climbed out, then helped Patsy.

Just as he reached for Grace a shot fired in the cellar. Grace cried out in the dark.

# NINE

Fire ripped through Grace's shoulder and she landed on the earthy cellar floor. Mold and rotting vegetables hit her gag reflex. She felt along the cool ground and found something glass…a jar. She chucked it at the assailant, then dove for him.

She toppled him and grabbed his wrist to keep him from shooting her again. She was certain it was a graze, but it burned like lava. Her pulse raced and sweat trickled down her temples, but she couldn't cower or cry. Her life was at stake.

He knocked her onto her back as they struggled.

Suddenly he was wrenched from her. Hollis dodged a fist to his face and defended himself with a punch to the shooter's ribs.

"Get up the ladder and get her out of here. Now! She has the keys."

Grace wanted to stay and help Hollis but he was right. Patsy was up there alone and with no training skills. She flew up the rickety ladder into a now drizzly rain. Dr. Sayer was crouched behind an old red tractor. "Come on!" Grace called. "We need to get to Hollis's truck."

Patsy nodded and Grace scanned the area. One was

in the cellar with Hollis. One was outside and one was still inside somewhere.

"Stay low," Grace commanded and started the trek from the house to the truck. Instinct told her stop. She paused behind a tree. Patsy's breathing was labored. The only way out of here was Hollis's truck. She'd disabled Judith Ryland's. Grace had no weapon. The attackers, who were fighting like skilled men, would have to know they'd make a break for it.

"We can't go to the truck. Is there any other vehicle on the property?"

Patsy shook her head. "Just a tractor but it's not going to go fast enough to get away."

Grace didn't see another vehicle either. The men after them must have parked somewhere else too. Where would she have parked if she was going to come in quietly? "Is there any other road beside the main one that leads to the house?"

"Behind the barn. A dirt road—for tractors."

"Where does it lead?" They were running short on time. Any minute they'd be ambushed. Where was Hollis?

"It leads to a gravel road that connects with another field but if you take a right it will lead you to the highway."

A tractor would be too slow, make too much ruckus and be seen over the cornstalks.

"Actually, there's a four-wheeler. Key's in it."

"Well, why didn't you say so?" Grace tamped down her temper. "Come on." She raced for the barn, keeping her eyes on the lookout. Inside the barn, she spotted a yellow four-wheeler. "Jump on." Hanging on the wall was a shotgun. "You ever use that?"

"No. I've never shot a gun in my life!"

Grace raced for the gun, checked to see if it was loaded. Two shells. Two shots. Something seemed familiar about this barn. She touched the gun rack.

A memory came! She knew exactly what to do.

Grace pulled on the gun rack and it opened. Inside a secret compartment dozens of weapons were displayed. All loaded and locked.

Voices sounded.

She grabbed two Glocks, a SIG Sauer and ammo along with another rifle—slinging it behind her back.

Patsy's eyes widened.

Grace didn't have time to be shocked. Everyone's life was at stake. She had to go on muscle memory and push the fear away.

Shoving the Glock 43 and the SIG in her waistband while keeping the Glock 17 in her hand, she cranked the engine with the other. Patsy was seated behind her.

The four-wheeler sputtered and died. She cranked it again.

"What about your friend?" Patsy asked.

Not in a million years would she leave Hollis behind. No matter how frightened she was, how rattled and jittery. She owed him her life and if it cost her everything to see him safe, then so be it. He'd do the same for her—had been doing the same for her. "We're going to go get him."

The ATV came to life. Grace's heart nearly beat out of her chest. Fear raced through her blood. Her shoulder stung like a swarm of bees and blood had seeped through her shirt.

But Hollis needed her.

As they sped from the barn, Hollis leaped from the cellar. One of the armed men toppled him to the ground.

Grace beelined it straight for them.

A shot rang out and Hollis flinched. A smaller man came around the corner, his gun trained on Hollis. Grace's heart jumped into her throat. She reacted, aimed. Fired.

The man fell to the ground, wounded but not fatal—as she intended. Hollis rose up and spotted Grace, then kicked his attacker's face, crumpling him to the ground. Hollis tore after the four-wheeler as the third shooter appeared with a rifle.

Grace fired first.

The man toppled to the ground. She couldn't be sure if he was wounded or dead, but their lives were on the line and she had to defend them.

Hollis jumped on the rails attached to the back of the four-wheeler, facing the killers. "Get the rifle off my back!" Grace screamed as she gave it full throttle, heading for the road at the back field.

Patsy scrambled and ripped the rifle off her back.

They were halfway down the road when Grace heard the sound of a vehicle.

"We got company," Hollis bellowed.

Grace fishtailed and weaved, sending mud flying.

"Steady, Grace!"

The pop of the rifle sounded and Grace glanced back as a black SUV veered off the muddy road and into the field. Guess they'd retrieved their hidden vehicle.

Taking the short window of opportunity, Grace turned into the opposite field and backtracked. They'd need the truck. A four-wheeler on a highway wasn't going to cut it in a car chase—or get them to Cottonwood in one piece.

Grace kept the four-wheeler as steady as possible. No sign of the men yet. Maybe the mud had them stalled out or stuck in the field.

As they neared Hollis's truck, Hollis jumped from the moving four-wheeler to secure their position—crazy how instinct told her that. Grace slammed on the brakes at the truck and practically slung Patsy from the ATV. "Get in!"

She opened the driver's-side door and shoved Patsy inside.

Hollis appeared and Grace bounded inside next, sitting in the middle. Hollis got behind the wheel and Patsy handed him the keys and he cranked the engine, then peeled out of the yard. "Well," he said, "that was quite the adventure."

Grace didn't know how he could be so calm and collected. She was a bundle of nerves ready to implode. She'd stayed in control under pressure but that was her exterior. Three men nearly killed them! One got a shot off on her.

"Grace, how's that wound?" he asked as he barreled down the gravel road and onto the highway. No sign of the killers.

Shoving her shirt over her shoulder, she inspected it. "Superficial. I don't think it needs stitches. Maybe a few butterflies."

He grunted and that's when she noticed some bruising around his right eye. "You okay?"

"I've been through worse. Patsy? You gonna make it over there?" he asked.

She only nodded and Grace held her hand and squeezed. "I'm so sorry about your friend. We…we can't go back. But we can call the police."

Patsy sniffed and wiped a tear with her free hand. "I'm used to losing people I love and not being able to say goodbye."

She must know about her sister's death. Grace's heart reached out for her. That would be unimaginable.

"I'm fairly certain those weren't Hector's guys. Which means they were likely trained agents. So…why do the people I once worked with want me dead? Any ideas?" she asked Patsy. "You know this Clive Epps that I worked for. Would he want me dead?"

Patsy rubbed her temples. She might be frazzled and not in the confiding spirit, but Grace needed answers. Her life—Patsy's life and even Hollis's—were in jeopardy.

"This whole thing is crazy. Where to even begin?"

"How about with why you were working with Hector Salvador?" Hollis asked, his voice low, wary and authoritative. He glanced in his rearview, then the side mirrors. Making sure they weren't tailed.

Was Patsy a bad guy too?

"I was forced to. My sister had cerebral palsy and needed special care. He threatened to kill her if I said no and if I said yes, he'd make sure she had quality care. I didn't have a choice. You know what he's capable of." A muffled sob escaped and Grace put her arm around her.

"I'm so sorry about your sister," Grace whispered. "We just found out she'd passed."

"Thank you. I couldn't stand not knowing how she was, so Judith went several months ago—to check on her. As discreetly as possible. I couldn't risk her getting caught. For all I knew Clive or Hector had Peggy under surveillance. That's how we found out she'd died a couple of months prior, but I couldn't do anything. Couldn't put Judith in a dangerous position." She sniffed and wiped her eyes.

How awful.

"I'm sorry for your loss," Hollis said. "I've lost loved

ones too, but I can't imagine not being able to be there when they…"

"Thank you," Patsy murmured.

"How long did you work for Hector and in what capacity?" Hollis asked and continued along the interstate, keeping careful watch.

"I'd been there almost a year when you came, Lucy. I was creating the toxin that nearly killed you."

"I'm actually going by Grace now."

"Grace," she said. "Then you were going by Valentina. I knew you looked familiar when you arrived on the compound, but I couldn't place you. It had been awhile since I'd seen a photo of you. But as time went on, I realized you were Henry and Lucinda's daughter. Imagine my confused state."

Grace glanced at Hollis. "How did I end up on a compound with Hector to retrieve a toxin from someone my parents knew? The world isn't that small." Was it?

Patsy sighed and leaned her head against the seat. "I knew your parents before they were married. Your father was a CIA agent, working bioterrorism at the time. They put together a task force comprised of agents and civilians. Geneticists. Pathologists. Biochemical engineers. That's how I met your mother. And your father. And Clive. He and Henry were colleagues on the task force—and best friends."

Grace shook her head, working to process everything. "My dad was a spy? Everything we read said he was a data analyst."

"No, honey. That was his cover."

Clive Epps could be the man who had been with her at the funeral. She described him to Patsy.

"Sounds like Clive."

"Did I tell you who I was when I came to the compound?" Grace asked.

"No," Patsy murmured. "You had no idea who I was and like I said, at first, I didn't know you. It was only after a few weeks that it hit me. I suspected why you came and that Clive probably recruited and personally trained you.

All this crazy knowledge, skills... Clive had taught her.

"How did we escape?"

"A man you knew came to the compound and you two got into a fight—physically. You torched the lab, took the research and we ran. He found us again in Miami. We lost him and took a private plane from there to Jackson, Mississippi, then you stole a car and we drove to Starkville where you had your farmhouse— you said no one, not even Clive, knew about it. You said once you confirmed the truth, you'd come for me."

Then she must have gone to Natchez after hiding Patsy and was intercepted by Peter Rainey near Cottonwood. Why would she be going to her mother's birthplace? To stash more research? Spread it out? "What truth?" Grace had stolen a car? Fought a man in Colombia and Miami? Who? Peter Rainey?

"That Clive was responsible for the death of your parents."

Hollis had driven the rest of the way to Cottonwood holding Grace's hand. After Patsy dropped that bomb, Grace had clammed up. Stopped asking questions. Completely retreated inside herself. She was on information overload and hanging by a thread.

Poor woman hadn't even had time to deal with the

three possible agents attempting to kill her—kill them all—earlier at her safe house.

He was waiting for her to implode and then explode. But so far, she hadn't. Instead, she'd trembled silently, and Hollis couldn't pull over and give her the solace she needed—couldn't embrace her. Instead, he'd called Cord and filled him in. He would call the authorities in Starkville. Questioning was inevitable, and statements would have to be given.

Hollis parked in Cord's driveway. He'd offered to put all three of them up and with what happened on the farm, Hollis wanted to keep this mess as far away from the inn and Tish as possible. The image of Judith Ryland falling to the ground replayed in his head.

Cord met them on the porch. He eyed Grace then gave Hollis a look. Yeah, he was thinking the same thing. She was a mess. "I might have some hot tea from when my sisters visited. Would you ladies like any?"

Patsy smiled. "Yes."

They made introductions. Grace remained silent. Her hair was matted with mud, and her face and clothing were filthy. "We'd like to clean up first, if that's okay," Hollis said.

"Of course."

"Thank you," Grace said and slipped her shoes off outside the front door. Hollis and Patsy followed suit and Cord led them to separate bathrooms.

After getting clean and dry, Hollis butterflied Grace's cut on her arm, but they barely spoke.

Cord had set out tea bags and a pink tea kettle sat on his stove.

Hollis raised an eyebrow.

"My sisters'. Scout's honor."

Hollis chuckled and helped himself to coffee, foregoing tea.

"It's an herbal blend. They said it was relaxing." Cord shrugged as if he didn't believe a word and would never consider finding out for himself.

Patsy and Grace poured themselves a cup. Grace added honey and then they sat across from one another. Hollis sat at one end of the table and Cord took the remaining chair opposite Hollis.

"Grace, do you want to talk?" Hollis asked.

She stared vacantly at the steaming cup of herbal tea with a fruity scent. "I don't understand. Why would Clive Epps want my parents dead? In my memory, we loved each other and he was terribly grief stricken. I need the story from the beginning."

Patsy sipped her tea. "I'll tell you like I did in Bogota. Your mother and I became fast friends and she and Henry had a whirlwind romance. One for the books, Lucy—Grace." She ran her finger around the edge of the thick brown mug. "Our mission was—is—classified. I can only say it was bioterrorism and we were working on a cure together. Once the assignment was over, Lucinda moved to Washington, DC, and married your father. I went to Bogota studying yellow fever with the CDC. Sometimes came back to Atlanta. Clive climbed the ranks in the CIA. Made powerful connections. Henry continued to work with him and then on other bioterrorism task forces. Lucinda and I kept in touch over the years."

"What makes you think Clive tried to kill my parents?"

Patsy licked her lips and stared into her cup. "Your mother confided in me that Henry was afraid Clive was involved in nefarious and traitorous activity—sell-ing bioterrorist weapons to the highest bidder for personal gain."

Hollis folded his arms and studied Patsy. He couldn't confirm or deny this story. But Grace was lapping it up.

"Not long after she confided that information, they died in the plane crash. I thought when I saw you at Hector's your mission was to eliminate me. Clive might be taking out everyone involved in that original task force who could accuse him of corruption, treason, terrorism. After a while, I confided in you about who I was and what I knew. You confronted Clive and he denied it all, but then that man came...he tried to kill you. I think Clive sent him to kill us both and retrieve the research and toxin."

"What exactly is this toxin? You've told me side effects but evaded much more than that. And don't say classified. I almost died because of it." Grace slid her cup of tea away; it was clearly not doing its job to calm her.

"It's a toxin with a water hemlock base. It produces cicutoxin. Hector wanted it turned into an aerosol to spray on rival cartels' poppy harvests. It would cause their buyers to become sick and they'd lose trust and come to Hector. But in higher concentrates—like you were blasted with and ingested—it would cause all the side effects plus foaming at the mouth, seizing before going into a coma and ultimately death. If this got into the wrong hands and was sprayed on agricultural crops in high concentrations then ingested it would kill millions of Americans and could easily crash our economic system."

Hollis and Cord both heaved a sigh. "Did Hector want it for that too?"

"No, he's a businessman. He's not interested in murdering potential clients or causing an economic crash. He was only concerned with knocking rivals out of the drug trade. That's why I kept things from my assistants as much as possible. They had no clue what we were really doing—what I was being forced to do."

Hollis wished he knew if Patsy was telling the whole truth—or even half the truth. If Grace believed the one man she trusted had betrayed her and killed her parents, then it would make sense for her to take Patsy and the research and run until she knew if Clive was diabolical or Patsy was a liar. Stashing the doctor and the toxin research—and possibly some of the toxin—in different locations was smart. That may be why she'd been running all over the country—not just to get away but to throw those after her off.

"If Peter Rainey was also a CIA agent on your team, and Clive sent him to kill you and take the research, he may have been the one to dose you with the toxin. That may have been the way he betrayed you," Hollis said.

Grace rubbed her temples. "Patsy, could you identify the man who came to the compound—who chased us to Mississippi?"

"Absolutely."

Hollis grabbed his cell and showed Patsy the photo he'd taken of Peter Rainey. "Is this the guy?"

"Yes," Patsy said and shuddered, then covered her mouth. "That's him."

That confirmed Peter Rainey was indeed a CIA agent and a colleague of Grace's. But he'd been clipped before he could help her or finish off what he'd started two years ago when he thought he'd killed her. Since the attacks on Grace hadn't let up, Hollis leaned toward the fact that Peter Rainey may have been coming to her aid somehow. That he was sorry for his betrayal, which could've been the attempted murder of her, and had figured out something was all lies and would have shared it had he not been assassinated.

A boom of thunder shook the house. Rain pounded the roof, cutting into his thoughts and reminding him the town was in danger if this weather didn't let up.

"Where are we on evacuations?" Hollis asked.

Cord waved him off. "That can wait for now…holding steady. This can't. What else do you know, Dr. Sayer, that can help us?"

Gripping the mug with both hands, she slowly shook her head. "I wish I had something. Grace was going to confront Clive. When she didn't return, I thought he'd killed her. Or that man who came after us had found and killed her."

Grace stood and paced the kitchen floor. "I thought of that too. Would someone I might be involved with or engaged to try to kill me?" She shook her head. "I think that earliest memory might have been an undercover operation together."

"Possibly," Hollis said. He wouldn't be upset about it, that's for sure.

Patsy yawned.

Cord stood. "I have a guest room upstairs. Second door on the left. If you need anything, let me know. I put more fresh towels in the bathrooms."

Patsy excused herself.

Cord cleared the cups and leaned against the kitchen counter. "Have you called the CCM team since you've discovered this new information?"

"No," Grace said. "I just need…to process it all."

"I'm going to bed, if you need anything, Grace, just knock," Cord said, and Hollis refrained from letting it irritate him. If Grace needed anything she could knock on Hollis's door.

Cord retired to his room on the west end of the house. One lamp in the living room glowed.

Grace collapsed on the couch and curled her feet underneath her. She took out a pad of paper and the silver pen she'd been carrying around since the first attack; she flipped a few pages and scribbled, continuing where she'd left off earlier.

He wasn't sure if she'd want company or not…but he did. He sat beside her leaving an inch or so of space between them. Leaning in slightly, he skimmed her list. She was adding to what she knew and what they suspected. She hadn't filled in the column of more questions, but it was longer than either of the other two lists.

"Now that it's just us, what are you thinking?" Would she be honest? Transparent. He wanted her to—to open up and lean on him.

"I'm thinking…the only person in this whole world I know I can trust without a sliver of doubt, Hollister, is you." She slowly locked onto his gaze, her eyes full of moisture. "You had my back today, and I knew—I knew that it was gonna be okay. No matter how much of my old training kicked in, no matter how terrified I was, I knew if you were with me, for me…it would be okay." She laced her fingers with his as if they were meant to be intertwined. "Tell me it's going to be okay," she whispered.

He'd been telling her. He meant it, but more than anything he wanted to show her. Her words ballooned in his heart, warmed shadowy, cold places. Would she… would she let him kiss her?

She held his gaze, searching. Her thumb rubbed the

tender spot between his index finger and thumb, sending a thrill along his spine.

He made a slow descent, giving her time to change her mind, to tell him to stop—that it was a mistake and he'd misread her signal, misread her need to connect—not to just anyone but to him.

As he cupped her cheek with his free hand, grazing his thumb along her high cheekbone, she shivered and gasped.

That was all the answer he needed, and he carefully, tenderly met her lips. They were as soft, sweet and wonderful as he'd imagined—the rare times he'd given himself permission. Her fingers slid into his hair, raining goose bumps from his head down his back. Leaning farther into him, Grace slipped her fingers from his and embraced him, holding tight, clinging to the promise he poured into her—to always have her back. To protect her. To fight alongside her. To always be honest with her.

Her vulnerability in the kiss dizzied his senses. This one glorious expression of their feelings for one another. This wasn't letting off steam. It wasn't a kiss laid with a foundation of fear and mistakes.

Her feelings were clear, and he reciprocated with gentle ease, patient yearning and hopeful restraint.

Before the warm moment fanned into a flame that might burn too hot, he gradually and begrudgingly brought it to a close. Pulling away only an inch, he smiled when Grace sat like a statue, eyes remaining closed and a tiny smirk on her lips, cheeks flushed.

She finally opened her eyes, her arms still encircling his neck. A satisfied smile filled her face.

"Was that okay?" he murmured.

"That was more than okay, Hollister Montgomery. And you know it."

The wonder on her face swelled in his chest as if she'd never kissed anyone before, and then it dawned on him. Grace didn't remember a first kiss. A couple of flashes of memory where two men she never loved—never truly cared for—had kissed her. Not the same.

This here, this moment, was like Grace's first kiss ever. The thought drove him to her lips again. Simple. Easy. Delicate. Then he pecked her forehead and she sighed and leaned against the couch.

"Hollister?"

"Yeah?"

She touched her lips, wiped her teary eyes. "If I had a whole self to give, I'd want to give it to you. I'd want to love you for my entire life."

The elation he'd just felt came crashing down in that one word: *if.*

"But I don't," she said and stood. "I don't regret those kisses. I do regret not being able to do it again." A small hiccup came from her and her bottom lip trembled. "I'm not free. I'm not sure I ever will be and that's not fair to you."

He wanted to argue with her. But she was right. She wasn't free—not of her past. And he couldn't be that freedom for her. No matter how many pep talks or re-assurances that her past didn't matter to him. No matter how many scriptures he quoted that revealed she was a new person in Christ. Until she believed it for herself, it was hopeless.

Only God could break through her fear, the deception that had her convinced she wasn't good enough—for God, or for Hollis. And even if she did break through that fear, even if she did give her heart to Hollis, when those memories came back she might change her mind and he'd be left picking up all the broken shards.

The reality was entirely too agonizing. Grace couldn't be his. Not now.

Maybe not ever.

# TEN

The clock read 4:12 a.m. Grace had gone to bed after leaving Hollis alone on the couch last night. She'd curled up under foreign sheets and blankets that smelled like Cord's house and not Hollis. His scent—though hard to describe—was in her memory. One she would remember always.

Those kisses.

It had been so much more than two people connecting physically. The past week had been one nightmare after another, and her only solid in it all was Hollis. He'd been there from the start of her new beginning. The first person she'd laid eyes on when she'd awoken from the coma. And in her mind, the first man she'd ever kissed.

Peter and Hector didn't count.

Except they did. How far had Grace gone for the sake of protecting her country? How many compromises did she make? What would come barreling into her consciousness when—if—she could remember again?

Surely nothing as pure, as beautiful, as tender as Hollister Montgomery's kisses. Nothing that could cause every nerve in her body to hum with joy and hope. Nothing that could heat her blood and skyrocket her pulse. Nothing that could make her feel as safe and cherished. She could still feel it, taste it.

Fresh tears fell.

Last night had been unfair to him. She'd been self-ish—she had a sneaky feeling she always had been.

Giving him those two wonderful kisses had been misleading. They didn't have a future together. They couldn't. The best thing for her to do was walk away, disappear.

This wasn't Hollis's battle to fight. It was hers. Last night all she wanted was Hollis by her side. Just him and her and the world. But how selfish was that? He could get himself killed. And even if they did get this whole sordid nightmare worked out, who was to say other en-emies wouldn't come for her? She might have dozens of people she'd double-crossed, angered...people who had scores to settle.

She gathered the pillows around her and stared out the window. Dr. Sayer had given her an overload of info. Clive Epps may have been responsible for her mom and dad's death. A man she thought she could trust—had trusted, based on the funeral memory.

A possible dirty agent.

Her vision blurred and a memory thrust itself to the forefront of her mind.

Peter Rainey was dressed in black, a dagger in his hand. His right eye was swollen and purple. Blood dripped from a gash in his head.

They stood on a bank, the muddy Mississippi roll-ing by. And it began to rain. That's why all this weather kept teetering on the edges of her mind as if trying to make a memory come.

"Don't do this, Noel." Noel! That was his real name! "Don't force me to kill you," Grace said.

"Always overconfident in your abilities."

Her body ached and multiple wounds Noel had inflicted on her ran with sticky blood.

"Not overconfident. Just confident I can end you."

"Going your own way can't help you now. It's caught up to you and is going to get you killed."

"I don't know what you're talking about, but if you mean killed by you...think again."

Peter raised the blade and Grace grinned and motioned him to bring it on. "Blades are my favorite. Should have shot me... Oh wait... I disarmed you. Twice."

"I want that toxin, Max."

"You and everyone else. This is your final warning or the last thing you're going to see is me standing over you in this dress...and the last thing you'll feel is my heel in your neck."

He hesitated. But then he made his move and came out swinging. Grace dodged the blade once, twice, then it sliced her side and she winced but kept fighting, kept moving. Peter—Noel—dove and toppled her to the ground, his hand sliding up the edge of her dress and retrieving the small can she'd strapped to her thigh.

"Max, you're so predictable. You should know I'm not polite enough to ask permission before a body search."

Grace grabbed his neck and squeezed. "I'll take your less than gentlemanly behavior and raise you an unladylike gesture." She kneed his groin, but before Grace could roll away, he pulled the small aerosol can out and smirked.

"Bye, Max."

Fear coursed through her veins. "Noel...don't do this.

You're making a mistake." She leaped to her feet, raised her hands in surrender.

"No, I'm following orders, unlike you." He blasted the spray and an indescribable burning singed her lungs as a bitter taste coated her throat. Her chest tightened and a splitting headache came on like a freight train. She was losing her ability to move; her body began to seize.

She fell to her knees. "Noel... Noel!"

His boot met her face and she toppled over the embankment.

The last thing she felt was the freezing water carrying her away and the unbelievable burning in her blood.

Grace sucked in a breath and tore the covers from her body as she jumped from the memory and the bed. Peter Rainey—Noel—had betrayed her by attempting her murder! He'd beaten her up and, in the end, left her for dead in the river water.

He was following orders.

Dr. Sayer must have been telling the truth. Clive sent Noel to murder her and take the aerosol and research to sell for his own dirty, personal gain.

She flew from the bedroom and smacked into Cord.

"Hey," he said. "I was just..."

"Just what? It's four thirty in the morning." She glared at him, that ball of rage rising with suspicion. He had no business lurking around her room this early—or at all. Even if it was his house. She might not be able to trust him. Anyone.

Grace's hand shot out and she squeezed Cord's neck and pushed him against the wall. "Just...making sure... you had towels."

He'd already told them they had fresh towels. He was lying. He'd come to kill her! Was he in on this too? She stepped in and continued to apply immobilizing pressure. "No one is going to get the jump on me again. Do you hear me?"

"Grace," Hollis's voice caught her attention. "Grace, let go of Cord or you're going to crush his larynx."

Confusion muddied her mind. Adrenaline flooded her veins.

"Grace," Cord said with a measure of raspy calm. "I don't want to hurt you, but if you don't let me go, I will."

"Grace," Hollis said in a hushed tone. "Let go, honey. You're safe. I promise you're safe."

One more squeeze and that'd be it for Cord—his threats were useless. She had him literally by the throat and instinct told her this would take a dinosaur down if necessary. She wasn't calling his bluff.

"Please, Grace," Hollis whispered.

Hollis. She could trust Hollis. Only him. She blinked then released Cord as the fog cleared and the fear subsided only to be replaced with utter shame. "I'm sorry. I—I don't know what happened."

The memory had triggered her mistrust, brought back old ways. The paranoia had been overwhelming. What kind of life must that have been? To be so on edge all the time?

"Please forgive me," she said.

Cord blew a heavy breath and rubbed his throat.

Grace couldn't force herself to look him in the eye. Or Hollis.

"Did you have another memory, Grace?" Hollis asked.

"Yes. Peter Rainey's real name is Noel. And he tried to kill me. He had orders. I assume from Clive Epps. He…he sprayed me with the toxin and kicked me into the water, Hollis. He left me for dead."

"I'm sorry," he whispered, but didn't come near to hug her. After last night, he apparently was going to keep his distance. Couldn't blame him. It would be smart—for anyone to steer clear of her. She was a ticking time bomb, an unpredictable mess. And everywhere she turned danger came for her full force.

"I'm gonna go on the porch and get some air." She slipped by him outside into the dank morning weather.

Fifteen minutes later, Hollis came outside and handed her a mug of steaming coffee. "Patsy just woke up."

"Glad she missed the show."

"I'm sure she's seen you in action." He inhaled deeply. "What are you thinking?"

Last night he'd asked the same thing and it had ended in kissing. That wouldn't happen today. "Hollis, in my memory, I told a man I was going to kill him. Going to impale him with my heel—that's kinda morbid. I didn't blink twice. And… I wasn't afraid of him. I knew I could take him and I didn't want to—but also it didn't seem to bother me that I was going to have to in order to save my skin."

Hollis sipped his coffee. "When I was on tours, I didn't bat an eye when I was surrounded by violence. I couldn't. One blink is all it takes, Grace, to go from living to dead. You don't get to feel guilty or afraid. You just have to do the job. And in that memory, in that moment, you were doing the job as well as defending yourself. He brutally broke you."

"In his defense, I brutally broke him too."

Hollis chuckled. "Anyone ever tell you you're a real bad-to-the-bone kind of woman?"

"Maybe," she teased, thankful for the lightness Hollis always disarmed her with. "I can't remember."

He playfully nudged her shoulder with his. "I'm sure

in memories that haven't surfaced yet, you feel deeply about what you did, not only to Peter Rainey or whoever he was, but to any human being. I know I did—do. But that's when I have to give it to God. Let Him heal and comfort me."

"It's hard to be healed when you don't even know all your ailments."

Like that fury that always boiled to the surface and begged to be unleashed from the pot, to spill out and scald. Like vengeance.

"God knows. And for now, that's enough. Once you recognize the ailment and the cause, then you get to decide what to do with it. You can choose healing— or not. God is always willing and ready if you choose the former." He tucked a hair behind her ear. "And as far as what you said last night... I agree. I shouldn't have kissed you at all. I don't regret the actual kiss. I don't even regret the emotion behind it. I just regret it because, Grace, it was powerful. And it's going to be tough to not think about it—or not to do it again. But I won't. We'll continue being what we are. I think that's best."

"Favorite friends?" she asked and tried not to die inside. Powerful. Perfect description.

"Absolutely. I'll take you to Tish's and then I need to help Cord with some flood issues. I won't be far and he's putting a deputy on the inn, so you have protection...or in your case, backup." He chuckled until it turned into a full-blown laugh. "Or just a bystander."

"I'm glad my skills amuse you."

"Woman, you are impressive in so many ways."

"Not intimidating?" she asked, loving that he didn't mind the fact she could be strong, as strong or even stronger than him. And he didn't mind when she was shaking in her boots either.

"Oh, honey, you're both. I love it all."

Love.

A wall of tension built.

He cleared his throat. "I need to get ready. We'll leave in an hour. Cord and I think it's best if he keeps Patsy lying low at the station. She's a flight risk. She may be telling you the truth, but I don't trust her, and it's smart and safer to keep some distance between the two of you."

Made sense. She nodded and swallowed the lump rising in her throat. Did he love all her ways or did he love her? The answer was embedded deep and it hurt too much to think about.

Hollis loved her.

And she loved him.

But they didn't have the opportunity to let it unfold— at least Grace didn't. If she kept hanging around, relying on Hollis for everything she'd keep him as trapped as she was now with no memory—no way to forge ahead into the future. It wasn't a choice for her, but it was for Hollis.

He deserved to fall in love with someone who could make a life with him. She had the love down. Just not the life. And he agreed with her—said it was best. But the feelings were still there and as long as she was here, there might always be a tiny drop of hope.

For once, she needed to do the right thing and let him have a chance at love. By some standards what she was about to do would be considered stupid. Cowardly even. But she didn't see it that way.

Leaving was brave.

Leaving was sacrificial. It released Hollis from the

prison of loving her and set him free to move on. Fall in love. Marry. Have a family. He might never be safe with her.

She needed to take this fight far away from Hollis, Tish, Cottonwood and all the people she cared about and loved. Hollis had no idea Grace was the flight risk.

Grace would take what she did know and dig for the truth. She'd keep CCM abreast but without including Hollis. Surely, she could trust Wilder Flynn to keep her whereabouts confidential. She had some savings from working at the inn; if she hired them, they'd have to. As of now, they were simply doing Hollis a favor.

But she wanted Hollis to understand. She headed for the guest room and grabbed the paper and pen she'd been using to compile lists and wrote him a letter.

In the truck, she slipped it into his raincoat pocket.

"I'll be here around noon for lunch. We're gonna need all hands on deck. Wilmington Road has flooded and the neighborhood behind it is in danger and needs to be evacuated."

She wouldn't be around at lunch. Grace fought the urge to cry.

Instead, she touched his cheek. "You're my favorite," she choked out and held his gaze. Not that she could forget those eyes and handsome face. Not in a million years.

He seemed confused and studied her a moment. "You're my favorite too."

She held her tongue for fear she'd confess how much she loved him and then he'd convince her to stay and maybe to try at a futile attempt to be a couple. Their first date would probably be interrupted by gunfire or bombs.

Grace exited the truck and hurried inside the inn before he saw the truth on her face. That was her goodbye.

Inside, she greeted Tish and donned an apron under the pretense of work. Once Tish was minding her own business and unable to see her leave or ask questions, she'd slip out. She grabbed a tray of pastries and entered the dining area. The crowd was slim. She set the tray on the buffet, turned and gasped.

Sitting at a table by the window looking right at her was the woman from an earlier memory. Her roommate. The friend who had warned her about Hector.

But was she friend...or foe?

Hollis tossed his jacket over his couch, rain dripping from it and creating a small puddle on his office floor. He checked the gear hanging on the hooks in case they got a call out and made sure they had a good supply of life vests on hand.

Even as he worked, he was completely unsettled by Grace's behavior and what she said before she jumped out of the truck. What was going on in her pretty little head? Had she recovered more memory and refrained from divulging? How bad could it have been this time?

Who knew where Grace was concerned?

He couldn't deny loving the Grace he'd come to know. Who she'd been didn't matter to him. The past was gone. But he'd had another thought late in the night when he'd replayed yesterday in his head. Grace armed to the hilt, riding around on a four-wheeler and defending all of them. The way she calculated scenarios. Had she gone to the truck instead of the barn for the ATV, she and Patsy would be dead. Maybe Hollis too.

She appeared to be in her element. Grace never once admitted to regretting that part. Only compromising situations and taking lives. What if her memory returned and she decided to go back in? Not every operative compromised their morals or their faith. She might want another go at it. Hollis couldn't blame her. But like Mary Beth, she'd leave for something that was more satisfying and thrilling than him.

That thought alone had kept him from barging into her bedroom in the middle of the night and fighting for them. Demanding she admit she loved him.

It was there.

In the kiss.

It was in her words. Her touch. The way she looked at him. The way she smiled when he entered a room. Hollis had ignored it, passed it off as nothing, but after the kiss he could no longer deny what he knew. Grace Thackery loved him.

Didn't mean she wouldn't leave him.

He wished he was still unaware about it—about his own feelings for her. It would make not being together easier. He had to determine a line, draw it and not cross it.

Find a way to be content with only friendship.

He went into his office and opened up his laptop. SAR training classes were coming up again and he needed to go over the volunteer applications, confirm the dates with Cord and send some emails.

His cell phone rang.

Cord.

"Hey," Hollis said.

"Levee broke, Hollis. Big trouble. We got vehicles floating down roads and people on the roofs of their homes. I've already called the Coast Guard. SAR isn't going to be enough."

"I'll send an emergency text out to volunteers. Where do you need me most?"

"Hope Glen apartments are in trouble. First floor is totally flooded and cars are underwater." A crack of thunder sounded, and Hollis felt it in his chest. "And another thing. I had to take my deputy off the inn. I'm sorry but I need all the help I can get, and let's be honest—Grace is quite capable of taking care of herself. I have a bruised windpipe to prove it."

No doubt, but Hollis wasn't underestimating agents or even Hector's men. They may have been called off, but they weren't gone. They were lurking. Watching. Hector wouldn't be so stupid as to let them pick up camp and move on.

"Patsy still at the station?"

"For now. But it won't be long and we'll be underwater too." His voice held a heavy dose of concern, but not panic. That was Cord, though.

"I'm heading to Hope Glen." He hung up and put his raincoat on. He patted his pockets searching for his keys and felt something in his right lower pocket. He retrieved a note. When did that get here? Hanging on to it, he found his keys on the desk and grabbed them in the other hand, then hurried to the training room to grab the extra survival packs he'd put together earlier.

Once he got the gear and the rubber boat loaded, he climbed inside his truck and opened the note.

Dear Hollis,

Grace must have put this in his pocket in the truck this morning. He continued to read:

I think I've known a lot of people and done a lot of things in my life. Most of which I don't remember. Some I do, and it's not pretty. You keep saying that God will work things out for good. I say He already has. The best thing that has ever happened to me—and though I can't remember the past, I just know it—is you. You found me that day. I'm glad it was you. I'm glad I've spent the past year and a half being your friend. Friends take care of one another. They look out for each other and they want the best for one another.

You've been the best friend. I have not. I've let you put your life in danger time and again. I've let you feel things for me that you shouldn't. Because I've needed you. I've been the bad friend, and that makes sense. I think I've been bad most of my adult life. Don't deny it. You know a blip of the things I've done. But I'm tired of being the bad friend. So I'm going to look out for you. Make sure that you get the best life, the one you deserve.

By the time you read this, I'll be gone. This fight isn't yours, and when it's over there's a huge possibility that a new fight will begin. We have no clue how many people want me dead for multiple reasons. We aren't sure if my memory will ever fully surface. There is too much uncertainty. Leaving will keep you safe as well as Tish and the town.

Don't worry about me, even though you will, I'm saying it anyway. I know more now than ever before. I'll figure it out. We both know I'm resourceful and good with a gun. Ha.

I'll never be able to thank you enough. But I'll always be grateful.

You'll always be my favorite.

Love,

Grace

Hollis's vision blurred from the moisture collecting in his eyes. Had she lost her mind? She was leaving? She thought going it alone was smarter, braver, better? Who would watch her back? The last time she went it alone, Peter Rainey nearly killed her. Granted, he had a bioterrorist weapon which gave him the advantage, but still.

Cottonwood with no Grace? Hollis with no Grace? He'd rather hang right here in limbo than be in a world without her.

The apartment complex needed him, but roads were flooding. Grace might not make it out of town. She could be stranded at the inn right now. He needed to get to her first and he prayed no one else did.

He rushed into the storm. Lightning flashed too close for comfort and he hopped into the truck. The road leading from the facility was almost under water. He had to go slower than he wanted so he wouldn't stall out.

Even Main Street was underwater. Fishing boats had taken the place of cars as families tried to escape. Was the whole town going to go under? Hollis parked and bounded out into knee-deep water as he slogged down the street and to Tish's inn. Water hid Grace's tires.

Tish met him at the door in waders. "Everyone is upstairs. We've got water everywhere."

"Where's Grace?" They'd deal with the mess later.

"She was here earlier, but when I finished upstairs she was gone," Tish said. "I assumed you'd come to get her."

How had she left town without a vehicle? Prickling went down his spine. "Did you see her with anyone?"

"No, but with all this rain and flooding, I've been preoccupied."

Now, Hollis hoped Grace had taken off like she said

and was safe. This flood was a prime opportunity to strike, though it would be difficult. Everyone, including law enforcement, was distracted.

"Hollis, what's wrong?"

"Probably nothing. Stay here, tend to the guests and call Cord to be evacuated. For now, there's a shop vac in Grace's place. I'll bring it to you and then I have to go." But where? Where would Grace be?

He went out the kitchen door into the rain. He trekked to Grace's house. The place was a disaster. Everything was in disarray. No way Grace would have done this. Did she come inside to pack and get ambushed? His heart jumped out of rhythm.

He turned and Crewcut came out of the blue. He drew his weapon. Hollis was too far away to disarm him. "You and me are gonna take a ride."

"I doubt that," Hollis said, calculating his moves. He inched forward. All he needed was to get close enough to get the gun, and if Crewcut wanted Hollis dead, he'd be dead. No, the guy from the shed the other day wanted Grace, which meant she'd either escaped or had been gone when Crewcut had arrived. Either way, she'd slipped through Crewcut's hands. Leaving might have been the smarter choice. Whatever it took for her to stay alive.

"I'm the one with the gun," he said.

For now.

Hollis inched a little farther as he spoke. "Lose Grace again?"

Crewcut laughed. "I don't lose anyone. I'll get Max. And I'm gonna use you to do it."

"We'll see about that," Hollis threatened.

"We will indeed." A new voice reached his ears.

Hollis turned and saw only darkness.

# ELEVEN

Grace perched on her chair at the Muddy Brewhaha. Public, but empty. With all the flooding, no one was having coffee. She cautiously watched the blonde who'd been sitting at the inn earlier. She now knew her as Siobhan. In her memory, she was a friend. Guess she'd find out soon enough.

Grace had refused to ride with her, so she'd slogged through the water in her knee-high rain boots and met Siobhan here. Away from the people she cared about at the inn. If Hollis came looking for her, he wouldn't come here. She was leaving town which meant stopping for a cup of joe wouldn't be on the to-do list.

Kali hollered from the counter, "The usual?"

Grace nodded.

Frowning, Siobhan pointed to Grace. "You look like a drowned rat, Max. But I get you don't trust me. You've never trusted anyone. I don't take it personally."

"My car was bombed so..."

"Wasn't me."

She didn't say it wasn't the CIA though. It could have easily been one of the three agents at the safe house, including the young one they'd dubbed Crewcut. Grace was as skilled in half-truths as Siobhan. Must have come with the training. "I have a million questions," Grace said.

Siobhan pointed a perfectly manicured, cherry-red nail at her. "I believe it. Let's see if I can answer them before you ask. How did I find you? Noel. Tracked him with a chipped pen."

A pen with a tracking device. She really was a spy.

Siobhan sipped the coffee. "This is good."

Did she realize Grace had no memory? She hadn't mentioned it or acted like she knew. Grace's mistrust seemed in character with who she'd once been. But if Grace was in Siobhan's shoes, she'd have done recon. Oh boy. That instinct. It scared her, mystified her and gave her a small thrill.

Grace wasn't up for small talk about coffee. "You tracked Noel."

"With the pen. The one Clive gave us all after our recruitment training." She leaned in. "Only works when it's writing, though. It pinged on Monday. Took me a day to get here. Been watching the inn where it was located, and you. I had to be sure you and Noel weren't in cahoots, but I haven't seen him. What'd you do to him?"

Like kill him? She said it as if Grace had no problem eliminating a person off the face of the earth.

Noel must have not realized he had a tracker on him. But they never found any pen or paper in his room… wait…the silver pen in the rooster holder. When guests left them behind, under beds or tables, Tish put them in the holder. Either she found it after the room was searched or Noel lost it in the inn and Tish found it. "Noel is dead. Sniper. Last Monday." It had been Grace using the pen that had sent the signal to Siobhan. Grace could only hope her old friend was telling her the truth.

Siobhan sighed and shook her head. "Who?"

Grace suspected the CIA, but Siobhan would deny it. She kept up the charade of having her memory. "Maybe Salvador's men. I assume they found me the same way Noel did." She told her about them coming for her but left out the part about Patsy. "Noel tried to kill me in Colombia." She relayed her newest memory as if it hadn't only recently surfaced. "I don't trust any of you."

"Noel was sent to extract you, the research and the toxin from Colombia. Hector was onto you. When he returned, he told us that you died in a lab fire with all the research and the toxin, and that Dr. Sayer must have escaped or been taken by the DEA. We had no reason not to believe him."

"He said he was following orders."

"He wasn't. Maybe he came to aid you but couldn't pass up a sweet opportunity to steal the goods and double-cross us all. I don't know. But why would Clive want you dead? He's the closest thing to family you have. Noel was always jealous of you, and he would have loved to hit you where it hurt most right before he tried to kill you."

Grace wasn't sure. She had no memory of her and Noel except the kiss they shared on what was probably an assignment. "So, Clive and all of you thought I was dead until the pen pinged?"

"Clive suspected Noel's duplicity when he disappeared about three months ago. He believes that Noel stole the research and toxin and was dangling carrots to buyers all along. When he went off the grid, Clive suspected he found one. We assumed then that Noel had killed you and you hadn't died in the fire. When the pen pinged…we thought we were chasing down bad guys. We found you instead. I assume Noel saw you on TV like you said and came to finish what he started since you could prove he tried to murder you. He'd lose it all. Go to prison."

Made sense, but Noel had seemed genuine and sincere. Again, they were trained to lie and to pretend. Grace herself had done it and fooled Hector, along with countless others no doubt.

"If that's true, then why did agents try to kill me at the farmhouse in Starkville?"

"How do you know Hector Salvador didn't hire mercenaries? He's a smart man. Coming after Mad Max? He would know better than to send gunrunners or average criminals." She grinned and sipped her coffee. "You'd have had them subdued in seconds."

Like the two men who'd blown her tire. She could have easily killed them. "It's possible." Grace wasn't sure who to believe. Everyone's story sounded plausible. If Noel was going to kill her, then what was all lies? Why offer to help her when he easily could have killed her like the sniper had killed him?

Grace closed her eyes and pinched the bridge of her nose, mentally counting to ten. "Patsy told me that Clive wanted me dead."

"That's old hat." She cocked her head and studied her. "Patsy isn't who she says she is, and just because she knew your mom and bonded with you on the compound by using her history with your mom doesn't make her an honest woman. She was working for Hector for money. A lot of it. She was afraid Clive was on to her and you were going to haul her in. She used your mom to get to you, and the Max I know would make her pay dearly for it."

Grace wasn't the Max she knew, though. "No, she was threatened."

Siobhan nodded, but her face was as sarcastic as one

could be. "Then why would Hector bother to pay her, if he could get her to work on a threat alone? That home her sister lived in was a pretty penny. We chased every rabbit trail that we could to find her."

She finished her coffee.

"Max, when are you going to come clean and tell me you lost your memory? It's obvious you are not the same. You haven't even asked about Magnum."

Magnum?

"Your cat."

"Oh. Sorry." She had a cat? Who was caring for him?

"You don't have a cat. Noel hit you with the toxin, didn't he?" Her voice gentled. "I'm sorry. But if you come with me, we can help you. We have skilled doctors who can bring your memory back. Clive has been going nuts."

"Why isn't he here then?" The bubbling anger rose.

"A softer approach was necessary. A woman. And we didn't know you had amnesia. We were following Noel." She scooted her coffee aside and took Grace's hands. "He was afraid you'd been completely brainwashed by Patsy and possibly Noel. You might have shot him on sight."

"I am not like that anymore."

"Of course not. Let's fix this memory issue and get you back to normal. I miss my roommate. My bestie. My colleague. We've got bad guys to fight."

Someone who could get her memory back sounded like a dream. But could she trust Siobhan?

Her cell rang. She braced herself for Hollis's call which she would ignore. Best to go cold turkey. But it was Cord and an eerie feeling came over her. "I need to take this." She answered.

"Grace, are you okay? Is Hollis with you?"

"I'm fine." Panic tightened her chest. "He's not. Why?"

"He didn't show up at the Hope Glen apartments. Thought he got stalled out. Wouldn't answer my calls so I suspected you might be in trouble. I saw his truck at the inn. Checked your place and it's completely trashed, and I found his cell phone smashed on the living room floor…and fresh blood."

Grace's entire world stopped.

She'd left Hollis to protect him, but leaving had put him in even greater danger. She'd never forgive herself for this. He might not either.

"What's wrong?" Siobhan whispered.

She raised an index finger. "I haven't seen him since earlier. Have you checked the SAR facility?"

"No."

"I will. I'm closer. Call if you find him." She hung up and relayed the message to Siobhan. "I'm going to borrow Kali's car. She won't mind." Although, the road was flooded; it would be tricky and maybe impossible.

"No way. This guy is important to you. I read it all over you. And no one has ever meant anything to you. So I'm all in, Max. Whoever has him, you have our full backing to get him. Let's go do what we do best."

"Okay." Grace only hoped her memory of Siobhan held true. They jumped up and raced out of the café, getting inside Siobhan's Jeep. "We'll find him. I promise."

"Thank you."

Whether she was proving she could be trusted for good reasons or more sinister motives, Grace didn't care at the moment. She'd take every stitch of help she could get and then some.

She felt nauseated. A headache coming on.

Hollis. Someone had hurt him. Taken him. It was all her fault.

They eased through the floodwater, Siobhan's vehicle handling the road pretty well. "Salvador's men must have taken him alive. Let that comfort you."

"Why?"

"Girl, you truly don't have your memory or you'd know why. To get to you."

"But I don't know anything."

"Sure about that?"

No. She had Dr. Sayer. They wanted her. Hollis was leverage—or they took him to cough up the doctor's whereabouts. If he told them they'd kill him. If he didn't, they'd kill him.

Grace's mouth watered as if she might vomit.

"Hey, don't get sick on me now. We have work to do."

Ten minutes later, Siobhan parked at the SAR facility. Grace felt worse by the minute. Sluggish. Stress and lack of sleep must be taking its toll. She pushed on. They entered the facility. "I'll check the office," Grace said. "You check the conference room. West side."

Siobhan nodded and they split up. Grace rubbed her head and tiptoed into the office. No sign of Hollis. After checking the bathrooms, training rooms—even supply closets—he wasn't to be found.

As she came into the open area where the diving equipment was located, a Latino man dressed in fatigues rushed Grace, knocking her onto the concrete flooring that was wet from the flood seeping in. Maybe Hector had paid mercenaries.

"Max!" Siobhan hollered and came running as another man charged her. She bent and flipped him, as Grace struggled to push her attacker away, but she wasn't focused. Everything was fuzzy.

Grace slid her hands across the floor, hunting for anything she could use as a weapon and her touch connected with an oar. She whacked her attacker and bolted outside, a gunshot echoed and Siobhan came running right behind.

"Get in the Jeep," Siobhan hollered.

But the biggest man dove onto Siobhan. She flipped him over, but he sprang up, a knife in hand.

Grace searched Siobhan's vehicle for anything she could use to help her.

Out of nowhere, she was thrust onto the ground, the cool water seeping into her clothing, soaking her hair. The man shoved her face into a puddle. Just like Monday. "No more playing around," he said in a thick accent.

She couldn't get her bearings. Her head was splitting in two and her stomach roiled, but she fought. Grace thrust out her leg and kicked him. He let up and she sucked in a gulp of air as he forced her down again.

Thunder cracked.

The bottom dropped out of the sky and torrential rain fell.

Lungs burned.

Need air.

*God, help me! Help me!*

Lately, the last thing she wanted was her memories. She didn't want to deal with the pain of who she'd been and what she'd done, but right now…right now she wanted it all. She needed her skill set, needed her training, and all her faculties to defend herself and to find Hollis.

He hadn't asked for this.

To save him, she'd take on every ounce of pain emotionally and physically.

Any second, she was going to pass out.

And like someone flipped on a switch, a loop of memories flooded her.

She was ten and disappointed Daddy had missed yet another birthday.

Sweet Sixteen. She'd had her first kiss. It hadn't been great. And of course, Dad had missed that birthday too.

Pain of her parents' death.

Clive! Her fatherly love for him when she hadn't had much fatherly love of her own. Dad had always been gone or distant. Mom had made one excuse after another.

And her training. All the extensive hours of special training.

Back.

Everything was back.

She arched her body like a cat in one swift motion and knocked the man straddling her off balance, then came out of the water with a vengeance.

He came at her again, but she blocked him and used her leg to sweep him on his back just as she spotted Siobhan come around behind him, and in a fell swoop, twist his neck and drop him to the ground dead.

The second man sucker punched Grace and she came at him with an elbow to his nose, then a move to knock him out. Instinct said kill him. One less bad guy in the world.

But no. That wasn't her decision. She was not God.

And neither was Siobhan.

Once, Grace would have snapped him like a twig and never blinked.

Hollis was right. She could choose her behavior.

"Going soft on me?" Siobhan snorted.

"He might know where Hollis is."

"Nah, he doesn't." Siobhan pulled her gun.

"Don't shoot him," Grace hollered. This wasn't the way it should be. Arrest him or something, but murdering him? Self-defense was one thing. Cold-blooded assassination. No way.

"I'm not." She looked at Grace as if she were out of her mind. "I'm not shooting anyone. Yet."

Before Grace had time to register what was happening, Siobhan raised the butt of the gun and everything faded to black.

Hollis blinked, his vision still spotty. Someone had knocked him out with a gun. The events slowly came into focus in his mind. The man who had gotten away in the storage shed had been there and a new...older man.

Grace... Grace!

Hollis couldn't stand. He'd been bound, hands behind him, feet tied to the legs of the chair. He was cold and wet. Quickly, he surveyed his surroundings. He was inside what looked to be a walk-in cooler. It was completely empty, but a milk jug was lying on the floor. Denner Dairy Farm.

The facility had been abandoned for about six months. No one had purchased it yet and Jerry Denner moved with his wife to Florida to retire. How did these people even know about this place?

CIA. They knew everything—had information at their fingertips in seconds.

The door was ajar and beyond it was the pasteurizing area. Machines. Tubes. They were on the edge of town—a town that was flooding by the second. Even if Cord went hunting for him, the last place he'd ever imagine to search was the dairy farm. And who knew where Grace was. He could only hope she'd fought off her attackers, escaped her home and run for the hills. In a perfect world, she was miles away by now.

Hollis pulled on the thin rope he'd been bound with. He'd tied many a tarp with this kind of binding. Someone had done a bang-up job. If he could get his knife from his pocket—though he couldn't feel the weight of it. They'd likely patted him down and confiscated his weapons when he was unconscious. They weren't idiots.

But he would find a way out of this. Find Grace. And they'd fix this somehow. Together. Who would believe one CIA agent with amnesia if she said her superior might be trying to murder her? Clive—any of them—could spin whatever tale they chose. Have her arrested. Worse.

Grace might not ever be free. She might be running her entire life. CCM might be able to help her disappear. That's why she'd written the letter. Hollis completely understood even if he strongly disagreed. She wanted Hollis to be happy, but she didn't comprehend the whole truth. Hollis would never be fully happy without Grace in his life.

He prayed God would rescue him, protect Grace and that He'd bring back her memories, even the tough ones. She would need them out there alone. She needed to know who to trust.

The door opened and the older man who'd knocked him in the head with the gun entered. Hollis had a headache as a reminder. "Well, nice to see you up and awake, Hollister Montgomery. Former navy SEAL. I got into your dossier. Quite the hero, aren't you?"

Hollis clenched his teeth and remained calm, assessing the situation and hatching a plan to escape.

"Born and raised in Alabama. One sister—Greer Montgomery who is engaged to be married to a Locklin

Gallagher, which means you have ties to Jody Gallagher-Novak and Wilder Flynn. Have they been helping you? Did they find Dr. Sayer for you? I know you have her."

"I have no one." On so many levels. "I'm sitting here in a chair alone."

The man only raised his eyebrows.

"You seem to know a lot about me. But I don't even know your name." He tried to remain calm, but they knew about Greer. Where she was. What if they tried to use her as leverage? What if they already had her— or baby Lin? Pure terror sent his heart into arrhythmia.

The man pushed his dark-framed glasses onto the bridge of his pointed nose which was slightly pink from being in this cooling unit. His hair was a little thin on top. Sharp chin. Thin lips. Icy blue eyes. Slender build, but Hollis had learned long ago not to underestimate anyone over size. Grace was a prime example.

"My apologies. Clive Epps." He smirked at Hollis's bound wrists. "I'd shake your hand…"

Hollis remained stoic.

"I'm not a bad guy—"

"Says the man who tried to kill me and Grace at least twice and has me bound in an abandoned dairy farm."

Clive chuckled. "I admit my first impression isn't great. But all this can be rectified. I just need Dr. Sayer. And I'll let you go."

And it would snow six feet in Mississippi this year. "I don't know where she is." That was the truth. She was at the sheriff's station but it might be under water this very moment, which means she could be at an evacuation site with a deputy guarding her. "Where's Grace? Her place was tossed. I know she didn't do it."

"No, she didn't do that. We were looking for something…that we didn't find. No matter. We'll get what we want. We always do."

"Where is Grace?" Hollis asked again.

"Grace isn't who you think she is, Hollister Montgomery. She's our Mad Max. A killer. For the good guys, of course. A wolf. This whole small-town charade. When she remembers—and she will—do you really think she's going to remain a part-time search-and-rescue volunteer? She's made for so much more than that. And you know it. She's vital to the agency. To our task force. A covert task force that most federal branches, including some of our very own, don't even know about. That's how lethal she is. How important. She's built for more than a one-pony show."

It was as if he'd reached inside Hollis's mind and pulled out his very thoughts. She was made for greater things. This town…him…they wouldn't be enough. "She doesn't trust you. She knows you tried to kill her."

"I did no such thing." Clive frowned. "Patsy Sayer used her vulnerability to turn her against me. I had no idea she'd been harmed or left for dead until one of our agents who tried to kill her—thought he had—led us here with a smart little device I gave him and my team. To keep tabs on them, make sure they were safe. I've scoured the world for her. It was like she vanished, hidden behind a veil that I couldn't even track."

"And now that you have, you've tried to kill us several times."

"No. I came for Patsy. For all I knew you and Lucy were aiding and abetting and harboring a fugitive. The agents at the farm had no choice but to do what was necessary in obtaining Patsy alive."

"Judith Ryland was shot dead."

"She was aiding and abetting. And Patsy is a criminal. In cahoots with Hector Salvador. I had every intention of arresting Patsy once Max had the toxin and research, but we lost her, thought Max was dead—"

"Quit calling her that!"

"But she is, Hollister. Surely, you've seen it come out in her. That wild cornered animal rage. I took that and channeled it into something beautiful. Something useful."

"You made her a monster under the guise of protecting America. You used her. She thought she could trust you."

"She can. You don't know her like I do. You don't know the anger and bitterness she felt when her parents died. I showed her how to use that to be the best. To avenge the death of her parents. To get revenge. I showed her how to wear the cloak of vengeance."

"Vengeance belongs to God," Hollis said through his clenched jaw. This man had taken a vulnerable, hurt girl, filled with hate, bitterness and revenge and warped her sense of right and wrong. Underneath all her failed memories, that wrath had been burning.

Clive closed the distance between them and leaned into Hollis's face. "We're all gods," he hissed. "We rule our own kingdoms and make our own paths."

"You're wrong," Hollis said. "And you're insane." Drunk on power. Maybe once Clive had been a decent man, but the authority and rank had corrupted him. Or maybe he'd always been this way.

"Am I?"

Rattling came from outside the cooling unit.

The door swung open and Crewcut barreled in with a chair identical to Hollis's in one hand and Grace slung over his shoulder like a sack of potatoes.

"Grace!" Hollis hollered. "If you've hurt her, so help

me when I come out of these binds—and believe me I will—you will regret it."

"Sounds like a man channeling some vengeance… some revenge. Maybe you're a little insane, too, Hollister Montgomery."

Hollis held his tongue but seethed.

Crewcut plopped a sleeping Grace into the chair and bound her. Her head hung, hair and clothes soaked to the bone. Muddy. A trickle of blood ran down her temple. She'd put up a fight. Good girl.

"Agent Larken is combing over Max's place now. Says she might find something we didn't." Crewcut shrugged.

"She's right. She and Max were roommates and best friends. She'd have knowledge you and I don't. But even if she doesn't turn up anything, we'll find Patsy and we'll get what we came for," Clive said.

Kneeling, Crewcut lifted Grace's chin and lightly smacked her cheek.

"Get your hands off her," Hollis growled and worked to get himself free.

"Calm down, boyfriend. I'm just trying to wake this little sweetheart up." He smacked a bit harder. "Max…" He whistled to call her attention.

She moaned.

"Yeah, got a little headache, huh? Wakie wakie. Time to play." Crewcut laughed, but Clive frowned.

"Memory or not," Clive said, "do not underestimate her ability." Clive smiled at Hollis. "Once we discovered she was alive, we did a little digging. Found her hospital records. Retrograde amnesia. Tragic. But we can help her. We have excellent doctors." He turned back to Crewcut. "Again, don't underestimate her. She still carries muscle memory and instinct."

Crewcut glanced at Clive and grinned. "To do what? She's bound."

In a lightning-fast motion, Grace raised the entire chair including her body and headbutted the arrogant jerk so hard he fell onto the floor. A small cut bled from above his eyebrow.

Clive clucked his tongue against his teeth and folded his arms. "Oh, something like that." He smiled at Grace. "Hello, Lucy."

Grace turned her attention to Clive. "My name is Grace."

"No, it's not and you know it's not by now, thanks to our mutual friend, Patsy, or possible memories that may have resurfaced." Clive came close, but not too close and slid her hair behind her ears, inspected the wound on her head. "Would you like some water?"

"I'd like out of these restraints and I'd like it if you let Hollis go. He has nothing to do with this."

"I agree. He doesn't. But you've made him a part of it. So he stays. I don't like this. This makes me look like the bad guy you seem to think I am."

"I don't know anything! I have amnesia!" Grace slumped and tears slid down her cheeks. "I just want this to go away."

Clive lovingly stroked her hair. "I know. But you're lethal and angry at me. So I have no choice but to do this the hard way. I'm taking you home where our doctors can get your memory back and then you will know the truth. You've harbored a terrorist, a woman guilty of treason. I'll forgive that. We'll move on. Accomplish our mission. And you will get revenge on those who killed your family like I've always encouraged you to do."

"I hear you killed my family."

Hollis watched, listened. Something wasn't right

with Grace. She wasn't much of a crier and the way she came at that agent—seemed more than muscle memory or instinct. Seemed calculated.

Clive sighed. "I loved your father like a brother." The conviction behind Clive's voice was believable. "And I love you like the daughter I never had. You know this— if you had your memory. We are family. All we have is each other. I never killed your parents, and I did not have a hand in it. But I know who did. And we've been tracking them for years. Bringing justice to these evil people and doing good for our country. Saving lives. Lucy, look at me." He waited for Grace to meet his eyes.

She finally made contact.

"I love you, Lucy. Let me help you. Give me Patsy."

"What will you do with her?" Grace whispered.

"See she's put in prison for the rest of her life so she can't recreate that toxin. We'll find what you did with her research and get it into the proper hands. Where is she?" he asked gently.

Hollis didn't like this at all. Even if Grace agreed and they took her with them, Hollis would be collateral damage. An eerie feeling said Grace might not make it out alive either. He worked the ropes, trying to loosen them. He could not sit here and watch Grace die.

Grace sighed. "I don't know where she is."

Clive's fatherly face turned to stone and he gave a small nod to Crewcut. "I hate to hear that. And I'm sorry for this."

Hollis's blood froze. He knew what was coming. "No!"

Crewcut made a display of curling his hand into a fist and reared back.

"No," Hollis bellowed.

The fist made impact with Grace's cheek. Hollis

didn't try to be discreet in getting loose. He worked while fear and adrenaline raced through him.

"Where is the doctor, Lucy?" Clive asked. A slight flinch revealed he might not necessarily like what was happening but this guy would go to any length for what he considered the greater good.

"I don't know. Please, don't do this," she cried. "I don't know!"

Clive gave the nonverbal signal and again she took a hit, the sound echoing off the walls into the freezing temps of the room, but Hollis blazed inside. His blood boiling. He wanted to tell them where Patsy was last, but the only thing keeping them alive was remaining silent and enduring the torture. Pure. Agonizing. Torture.

Another clip to the chin. With every bit of contact, her face reddened, bruised. Her bottom lip bled.

"One more," Crewcut said, "and we'll go to something far more painful."

Grace's chin rested against her chest. She said nothing.

Silence permeated the room.

Had she taken too much? Had he broken her?

Hollis's breath caught as an invisible charge filled the atmosphere and he studied Grace.

Slowly, her head lifted and she stared Crewcut in the eyes. "You have at it, big boy," she said softly but menacingly. "You don't know pain but I'm gonna get a turn real soon…and you *will*." She licked the corner of her lip and held his gaze; his cheeks blanched. Even Clive was taken aback.

This was the wolf Clive described. The machine he'd built.

But this was not Grace. Not the new faith-filled Grace. "Grace," he murmured.

She turned to him. "Just hold on, Hollis. Won't be but a minute now." She grinned and winked.

Grace had her memory! It was there in her eyes. All her training. Her cunning. Her skills. And everything in between.

But they were bound and he'd been a SEAL and wasn't able to break free of the bindings. What made her think she could?

"Please don't do something stupid," Hollis begged.

"Enough!" Clive's bark cut through the room. "Nice to see you, Max." He seemed disappointed. "She won't talk now. You can beat her to a bloody pulp." He gestured with his thumb toward Hollis and Crewcut moved over. "You want to know why you're here, Hollister Montgomery? Contingency plan." He nodded and Crewcut went in with a strong uppercut. Hollis's head rung.

This was gonna be a long night.

# TWELVE

Grace braced herself, but kept an unemotional expression plastered on her face. Inside, she was screaming and crying for Hollis. Clive was right. This brave, wonderful man had been brought into her mess. He knew enough to know that Hollis meant something to Grace.

Siobhan had said she'd been watching Grace for a few days. She'd seen her interactions with Hollis, and having known her before the amnesia, Siobhan knew there were deep feelings involved.

But Crewcut and Clive didn't know how deep. That gave Grace a sliver of a fighting chance to stop this, and she would.

Blood poured from Hollis's nose, down his chin. The young agent wasn't someone she knew or had met before. But he was clearly enjoying the beatdown.

"This could all be over, Max. Just tell me where she is," Clive said.

Grace held her emotions in check. When her memories had flooded in, it had been overwhelming. All she'd ever done. Been.

The day Clive told her the truth about what he did for a living. What her father had done. Why he'd missed so many family events, important dates in her life. The distance she had always felt. She'd been furious with her dad for years and that day she learned the truth, she couldn't even tell him how sorry she was for the times he had reached out and she'd rejected him—put up a wall so he couldn't hurt her again. That anger had held her back from following in the faith she'd been raised by Mom to have. She'd been furious at Dad and God. And she'd turned away from both.

Until her amnesia when she'd forgotten she'd had misplaced anger directed at her heavenly Father and with a clean slate, given her life to Him.

That guilt had been heavy. So heavy before the amnesia. The frustration at Mom for not telling her the truth but making excuses had been unfair, but when Grace became an agent, she understood. Her kind of work—Dad's kind of work—was a secret to everyone. The only reason Mom had known was because she'd been on a task force with him at one time.

Clive had recruited Grace and promised they'd find who was responsible for crashing their plane and he would help her get revenge. She unleashed that rage and used it to be at the top of the game. Strong. Lethal. Cunning and powerful. Every time she'd kissed her locket before taking out a target she'd been told was involved in their deaths, she'd been kissing them. A locket she'd never been able to open, even before the memories faded away. She'd assumed it had only looked like a locket and wasn't meant to be opened. Now, she was glad she'd never destroyed it. It would have been pointless!

"You do what you think is necessary." She had to pretend she didn't care about Hollis and trust that he knew the truth. Understood the gravity of the situation they were in. Clive wouldn't stop until he had what he wanted.

He was telling her the same story as before she lost her memory.

So was Patsy.

Grace wasn't sure who was telling the truth then or now. That's why she'd escaped the compound and hidden Patsy—to gain the truth for herself. If Patsy had lied, she'd go to prison. If Clive had, then Grace would have worked tirelessly to gain the necessary evidence to have him put away. She never had the chance to dig.

Noel had shown up after she hid Patsy in the safe house she'd purchased under a fake company name and hid from everyone. Being an agent had led her to extreme precautions and heavy paranoia. She'd been on her way to Natchez—since it was only a few hours— to visit Mom and Dad's gravestones. Grace felt Mom would want to be at rest with her own parents. She had talked about them often. And Dad would want to be with Mom. No bodies, but they'd put the markers there and Grace wanted to put down flowers.

But Noel had found her outside of Cottonwood before she could get to the cemetery—get to the work of uncovering the truth.

She might have lost the toxin that day, but she still had the research, and now with her recovered memory—she knew exactly where it was.

Hollis took his punishment in silence and Grace looked on as if it didn't faze her. Clive held up his hand for the younger agent to stop. "What's a few punches, right, Max? That's kindergarten."

Oh no.

She kept an uninterested glare on Clive.

"When did your memories return?" he asked.

"Today. When Hector's men tried to drown me in a mud puddle. Bit insulting. Right before Siobhan got the drop on me. In my defense, I was still hazy from the drug she clearly slipped in my coffee to slow me down. What did you tell her that would make her turn on me? Knock me out. Let this young idiot pound on me." She worked to keep her voice from shaking, her legs from bouncing in fear. Fear for Hollis. Clive would kill him. There had to be a way out of this.

"She knows you're confused. She knows you have killer instincts. None of us enjoy this. None of us like to see you this way, but what have I always taught you? Taught all of you."

"Anything by any means for the greater good."

"That's why Siobhan is willing to hurt her closest friend. She will regret it later, I'm sure. As we all will." Clive moved behind Hollis.

Grace feared he would break his neck.

He knelt.

"All your memories?"

"Enough." Yes, all of them. Every shameful thing she'd ever done. Every hurt, disappointment, regret. Every dastardly deed. But now was not the time to fall to pieces over them. God would help her through it. Every scripture she'd read, every word of hope from Hollis and Tish were right there in the mix.

Yes, she told the agent she would make him pay and it would be painful, and she couldn't deny wanting to hurt him for hurting her, but it was mostly a scare tactic. She was not Mad Max bent on revenge. She was Grace Thackery now. A new creation in Christ. She'd chosen not to kill Hector's man, but she could have. She would not hurt the agent, unless she was forced to protect herself or Hollis.

And she would not kill Clive if it was true that he was responsible for her family's death. Nor would she kill Patsy.

She wanted to heal. To be free. And if all things were possible through Christ—then she could. Would. And she knew that they were. She believed every word of scripture.

Clive took Hollis's hand. Hollis's jaw twitched, clearly anticipating what Clive was about to do.

Dread filled her gut.

"Maybe you don't know where Patsy is at the moment. The whole town, including us, is almost under water. A real mayhem. Coast Guard is out there and everything. But you know where she was last. Just tell me."

"I'd rather not."

With a quick snap, Clive broke the bone in Hollis's middle finger. Blood whooshed in Grace's ears. Hollis didn't even flinch. That was her navy SEAL hero. Strong. Brave. Tough as nails. Solid to the core. Would he be able to forgive her for this? When all was said and done, he might ask her to go. She had deadly enemies—all over. Any one of them might decide to track her down for a vendetta. He'd be right to be done with her. Her heart sank as low as it could go.

How much more of this could she endure? Seeing Hollis broken for her...

Clive's cell phone rang. He answered, listened then grinned. "See you in five." He stood and moseyed in front of the chairs, talking to the younger agent. "Chopper's waiting at the Lander's field. Can we drive out of here?"

"We got a Coast Guard RIB."

Rigid inflatable boat. High-speed power. The flooding must be even worse than before Grace had been knocked out by Siobhan—where was she anyway? And why leave now? They didn't have any information.

"It appears we don't need you to answer. I have what I need." He turned to the younger agent. "Get the RIB ready. I'll join you in a minute." After he left the cooling unit, Clive sighed. "By the way, Siobhan said to tell you that you'll no longer be able to wear those red heels."

No. The world tilted. Siobhan found the heels she'd been wearing the day Noel had tried to kill her. The last thing she wanted was to not have the flash drive on her person and that meant wearing the shoes, but she was accustomed to being in heels for long periods of time in many undercover operations. This time, she'd added the dress and had planned to sweet talk a set of keys from one of the used-car salesmen for a test drive alone. If he was distracted by her looks, she had a better shot of gaining the keys and stealing a car. But Noel had found her first.

It had all gone downhill after that.

Those heels. The right heel came off the shoe and revealed a secret flash drive attached. Grace had stored all of Patsy's research and notes before burning the lab to the ground. Not to hide it from the DEA, but to keep it from Hector, Clive and even Patsy. Now that Clive had it, he had everything to produce the cicutoxin component that could destroy millions. If he was crooked, like Patsy said, then he would sell it to enemies.

"What are you going to do with it?" Grace asked.

"What I do with everything. Keep it safe. Out of the hands of those who would hurt Americans. I'm not the bad guy, but you have forced my hand."

"And Dr. Sayer. You'll leave her be now?"

"No. She's a criminal. And we already have her.

When the town went under water, they evacuated to higher ground and into neighboring towns where flooding hadn't occurred yet. She was among them."

"Not alone. She'd have a deputy guarding her."

"There are always causalities in war, dear." Clive started for the door, then turned back. "Would you come willingly with me? I'll forgive all you've done."

"All I've done!" What about the maiming and torturing and killing Clive had done? Even now, Grace still didn't know the whole truth. But she couldn't believe Clive. Not when he'd hurt her, hurt Hollis. Murdered an innocent deputy. Judith Ryland.

"Go with him," Hollis said.

"What?"

"Go. I'll be fine."

"No," Clive said and pulled his gun. "You'll be dead either way."

"Don't!" Grace hollered. "I'll go!"

"You're only saying that to keep him alive—it won't. He knows too much. And if you won't come to be loyal, then you're a liability."

Grace had to do something. Quick. He would kill them both. "Wait. If you're going to kill us, then at least tell me the truth. Please. Did you have anything to do with my parents' death?"

"I did not kill your parents. Do you want to go first so you don't have to see Hollister die?" he asked as if asking her to choose a flavor of ice cream. "I'd give you that gift."

Suddenly, Hollis burst forward, knocking Clive to the ground. The gun clattered to the floor. Hollis's chair broke and he slid his feet free, kicking the gun across the room. His hands were still bound to the chair.

Clive jumped up and kicked Hollis backward then raced out the door and slammed it shut.

"Hollis! Are you okay?"

He used his weight to slam the chair down again and it shattered, but his hands were still bound. "Can you get me loose if I come behind you?"

"I can do better than that," Grace said. "I have a knife strapped to my right calf."

"I could kiss you," he said, his face was streaked with blood and his left eye had started to swell. He sat on the floor, his back to her, but he couldn't get his hands higher than her ankle. He growled.

"Move out of the way," she said.

Hollis scooted forward.

Grace shivered and spotted the vent. Icy air blew heavily from it. "Did they—"

"Drop the temp? Yeah. They're gonna try to freeze us to death and we're wet, so it won't take long."

Grace used that fear and rocked hard in her chair until it tipped backward, jarring her head. Her arms screamed in agony at the odd angle she'd forced them into. "Get that knife, Hollis."

Hollis slid his hand up her pant leg and unsheathed the knife, cut himself free then sat Grace upright and freed her.

The second she was unbound she threw her arms around his waist and clung to him. "I was so scared. I'm so sorry I let them do that to you. You have to know it was killing me."

He cradled her face. "I know. You did what you had to. I'm proud of you, Grace. Do you truly have all your memories?"

She nodded. He was proud of her? That was not what she expected to hear. "Clive and Patsy are telling the same stories they did two years ago. But either way, Hollis, I don't trust Clive. He killed Judith Ryland and whoever was guarding Patsy. That's taking innocent lives. We have to stop him. We have to rescue Patsy and get that research." She told him how it was stored in her heel and how Siobhan duped her. Every bone in her body had turned to ice.

"We got to get out of here," Hollis said. "Now."

Grace clutched her locket and kissed it for good measure, an old habit. But no longer did she need a locket to help her out. She had the power of prayer.

Hollis worked on the door but it wouldn't budge.

Scanning the room, Grace's eyes landed on some tools in the corner. She searched for anything that would work to get them out but found nothing. The temperature continued to drop covering her in goose bumps. She worked to focus on something else besides that—a tactic learned in her training with Clive.

"Grace," Hollis said and pointed upward. "Vent. It's too small for me, but you could get up there. Get out and open the door. But…you'd have to fight the glacial air, push against it to the main vent, break through. It's dicey."

It was their only shot. She ripped his rain jacket and wrapped her hands in the material like mittens for some protection against the biting air blaring at below zero up inside there.

"Give me a boost."

Hollis cupped his hand and she put her boot in it, but he didn't hoist her up. Instead, he searched her eyes. "I want you to know that letter… I do not accept it."

Now wasn't the time to discuss it. "Boost me up."

"Promise me you won't give me the slip once you open that door."

She touched his cheek. "I promise. Time's ticking, Hollis."

He lifted her and she punched the vent until it gave way, then she hauled herself inside, her body protesting in pain.

"Hollis, if I don't make it out—"

"Don't even say such a thing." His voice and eyes adamant.

"I'm being realistic."

"Time's ticking, didn't you say? Get up there. Get to the door. Get me out," he said through chattering teeth.

"And think warm thoughts?"

"Tropical beaches. Roaring fires."

She sighed and crawled through the icy vents. Her toes went numb.

Her fingers.

Couldn't think straight.

But she pushed through, searching for a way out. A way to Hollis.

She grew tired.

Her muscles stiffened.

So…tired.

Her hair felt stiff, frozen against her skin.

Hollis paced the freezer, anxious and also to keep warm, but it wasn't working. He was freezing and warm thoughts had long been buried in icy pain. That kind of frigid air blowing full blast…if it was a far crawl… Grace could die of hypothermia in there. And he wouldn't be able to get up there and rescue her. After she'd gone up, he'd splinted his broken finger best he could with what little he had to work with. Now he chewed on his thumbnail, aggravated that he was stuck in here and unable to help.

Grace was alive at least. Would she have to run and go underground? Would she be able to save Dr. Sayer? Would anyone believe her when she claimed Clive had a deputy murdered? Grace knew Clive better than anyone and if she said he'd eliminated him, then he had. But it was an upstanding agent's word—and his cronies following orders—against hers. They could twist it any way they pleased.

Their situation hadn't changed. Even if Hollis begged to run with her, she wouldn't let him. She would give him the slip. Tell him to make a life here and forget her. It would be safer—but would it? If Clive Epps realized that Hollis was alive, he'd come to finish what he started. He wasn't out of the woods.

Grace may not be either. *God, please let her be alive.*

A noise caught his attention and then the door opened. Grace stood before him, broken, bloody and nearly frostbitten. Her lips were blue and her hair was like a sheet of ice. "If you ask me what took so long I might snap your other finger," she teased through sheer exhaustion.

"Now that you remember how?" He returned the banter, never more thankful to see her in his life. Their bodies were nearly at a breaking point—Grace's even more from crawling through cold vents. He hauled it out of the freezer and they raced through the flooding pasteurizing plant.

Outside it was pouring rain but at least it was warm. If Grace kept moving, she wouldn't suffer any serious effects from being inside the ducts.

Everything within their eyesight was a water world.

"We can't drive in this."

"We need a boat," Grace said.

Hollis stared past the dairy to the old farmhouse

barn. "Denner liked to fish. We might catch a break and find a boat in there."

Grace snorted. "A johnboat with a trolling motor? We need speed."

"Or—" Hollis grinned "—we just need good geography." He sprinted toward the old barn and Grace caught up with him. It was like she had hidden energy in places that popped out at unexpected times. The way she pushed herself—the strength within her—mesmerized him. This woman was the most incredible person he'd ever known.

They reached the barn and ran inside where it was at least dry overhead. In the corner, something was covered with a tarp. *Please be a boat.*

Hollis tossed off the tarp to a River Jet bass boat. "Praise You, Lord!" Hollis pulled and Grace pushed the trailer it was on out into the rain and hauled the boat into the water.

Grace ran back inside and came out with a gas can. "Just in case."

"Look at you knowing things now." He winked and she actually laughed then groaned as her lip cracked and began bleeding again. The fury at what that man had done wanted to be released, but Hollis wasn't after vengeance. Only justice.

He got the motor going; it sputtered then roared strong. No life vests. No time to find them. "What's this talk of geography?" Grace asked.

"We have an advantage. If everything is underwater," he hollered over the rain and the motor, "we can take a shortcut to Lander's field. Beat them there even. Pays to know the lay of the land like we do."

"We need weapons."

Hollis patted his side. "I've got Clive's Glock. It's locked and loaded."

"Yeah, well, I got nothing." She rummaged through the boat's compartments and seat benches that doubled as storage. She held up a filleting knife. "It'll slice. I can work with it."

"I'm sure you can."

He cut a hard right, floored at how quickly the town, even the outskirts they were on, had been submerged. The governor would have to declare a state of emergency.

"How is this going to go down, Grace?"

Grace sat in the seat beside him. "Hopefully, not bloody, but it's Clive. I don't want any more death, Hollis. I'm sick of bloodshed."

"What about being an agent?" He had to ask. Had to know if that love and passion for it was still there.

"I love being an agent. I love protecting our country. But I don't love the things I did, Hollis. And there were a lot of things. I don't want to talk about it. I need to focus. We're outnumbered three to one, maybe four if the pilot is an agent. I have no idea where Patsy stands or even if she's with them. Or alive."

"If he is corrupt and did have a hand in your parents' deaths, he'll get rid of her just to shut her up."

"He will. We need to save her."

"If she's alive, we will."

A blue chopper came into view, the blades already whirring. It began to rise into the air.

"Get closer," Grace called and stood on the edge of the speeding boat, hands out balancing against the bumpy water and wind from the chopper.

"What are you gonna do?"

"What we're gonna do. We're taking a flying leap, Hollis."

She'd lost her marbles and he loved it. Full throttle and he sped toward the copter as it continued liftoff.

"Closer!" Grace put the handle of the knife between her teeth to hold it, keeping her hands free.

Hollis kept one eye on the aircraft, gun in hand.

Gunshots fired and Grace ducked, then leaped into the air and grabbed ahold of the landing skids like she'd done it a thousand times.

Hollis returned fire, but needed to conserve bullets. He edged the boat farther, then jumped from the captain's chair onto the other landing skid while Grace was already pulling herself up to make a charge into the birdie.

Crewcut leaned down but Grace was faster, swinging upward and kicking him square in the kisser and flinging herself inside.

Hollis lifted himself up as Clive aimed a new gun on him. The chopper veered and Clive lost his balance. Hollis swung into the seating area and launched himself on Clive as they struggled for the gun. Grace and Crewcut continued to tangle, and Dr. Sayer sat with her mouth hanging open. At least she was alive.

Hollis spotted cuffs lying on the floor. He made a play for them, elbowing Clive in the nose, then he flipped the agent over and cuffed him right as Crewcut threw Grace from the helicopter.

His heart stopped.

In two moves, he had Crewcut unconscious and had fallen onto his belly to peer out. Grace was hanging on to the landing skids with one hand.

Hollis reached out. Couldn't quite connect. "Stretch, Grace!"

Rain poured. He could see her fingers slipping.

No. No. He couldn't lose her. Not after they'd come so far. "Stretch," he roared. He hooked his feet under the seat and slid out of the helicopter, hanging freely. If Crewcut woke, he was done for. Grace too.

Grace shouted, "Get inside. I can't... I—"

Just as her hand slipped, Hollis grabbed ahold of her wrist and hauled her up until she could reach the floor of the helicopter and push herself inside. Hollis slid in beside her and sighed relief.

Clive stood above them—free of cuffs—and pointing a gun.

# THIRTEEN

Grace worked out the scenario quickly. The young agent was out like a light on the floor. Patsy remained silent—possibly in shock—in the seat. The pilot was cool as a cucumber. Probably an agent who knew as long as he kept them in the air, he was safe.

Clive had a gun on her and Hollis, moving it from one to the other.

The knife was on the floor and no doubt the pilot had a gun. Could she get to him without getting shot? Probably not.

"I should have had Agent Foyles shoot you," Clive said.

"I love you too," she countered, sounding entirely braver than she felt. At least Crewcut now had a name.

This was it. Hollis had no idea the day he did a good deed by rescuing her that he'd all but signed his own death warrant.

But he had rescued her. From much more than death. From a life that never truly fulfilled her, from a path that would lead only to destruction. Because he'd led her to church that first Sunday after she'd awakened from the coma. And ultimately into the arms of her real rescuer—Jesus.

"I'm sorry, Hollis," she said.

"For what?"

She half laughed. "Clive, you have murdered innocent people. Judith Ryland. The deputy guarding Patsy. And you attempted to murder Hollis who had nothing to do with any crime. Neither did I. You can't get away with this."

"And Lucy's family," Patsy said. "Tell her, Clive."

"Shut up, Patsy."

"Tell her how you found out that her father was looking into you after the toxin you recovered fell into Russia's hands along with the antidote we'd created thirty years ago on that special task force. Tell her how you lied and said it was me. That I did it and you had 'eyes' on me. But then other projects were compromised that I didn't work on at all. Henry suspected you. He was coming to me in Bogota—bringing Lucinda with him. A vacation with a hidden agenda to keep you from discovering his real intentions, and you found out anyway and made sure that plane went down before it ever reached me."

Grace held her breath. "Is that true?"

"That your dad might have suspected me in one of his investigations? Possibly."

"Liar!" Patsy screamed and shook her head. "It's all over now. No point in either of us lying to her anymore."

"What did you lie about, Patsy?"

"All your mother told me was she and Henry were going to Costa Rica on a nice long vacation and since they were close to Bogota, Henry suggested they come and see me too. She had no idea about Clive and what Henry suspected. I made that up to get you on my side. But the minute she said Henry suggested they visit—I knew. He was coming to question me. I wasn't sure if

Clive was afraid I'd tell Henry the truth about himself or if he just didn't care and wanted us both dead so we could never talk."

Clive turned the gun on Patsy. Hollis dove onto Clive, knocking the gun to the floor. The pilot reached across the seat and Grace bolted into action, grabbing his gun and pointing it on him. "I don't think so."

Hollis pinned Clive.

Patsy snatched the gun and aimed it on Clive. "It's over, Clive. For us both." She turned to Grace. "I knew what was really going on because I helped him do it that first time thirty years ago, and then over and again through the years. We've sold bioweapons to terrorists all over the world."

"Why would you do it, Patsy?" Grace asked.

"For the money. To help my sister. Clive...he was just greedy. But I knew he'd kill me when he was done with me. So I took measures into my own hands. I kept proof of his involvement and sent it out to several different people I trusted. They didn't know what they had. I made sure of it."

"Shut your mouth!" Clive hollered.

"But Clive knew that too. He went on a treasure spree, collecting the evidence I had against him. People began turning up dead. I knew I was in trouble. That's why I took a job with Hector, for money yes. But the main deal was protection. From Clive."

Grace went into her memory. Hits she'd made. Intel she'd retrieved. "Did you send this evidence to Canada, the Cays, India, Tokyo?"

"Yes," Patsy whispered.

All places Clive had sent her on missions. All targets that he said had a hand in murdering her father and mother. Lies. Like Noel said. She'd blindly trusted the only man she considered family. And if Clive had ordered Grace to kill Patsy in Colombia, she would have. She'd trusted him with her life, like all the others on the team. "When I questioned you about my parents and your involvement, you knew then I'd do whatever it took to find the truth. You did send Noel to kill me, but you had to have lied to him or he wouldn't have crossed me. What did you tell him? That I was betraying our country and going rogue?"

Clive's face said it all. That's exactly what he'd done.

"Noel came back. Mission accomplished, but Siobhan said Noel told everyone I died in the fire." Why? The truth smacked her. "You told Noel to lie about my death to honor me. You loved me too much to let me go down as a traitor to our country, and he agreed because at the end of the day, Noel was my friend, but duty to the job came first."

Clive closed his eyes. "You only had to trust me."

"I did." Until she couldn't anymore. "Noel dropped off the grid not long ago… Something must have not sat right with him. Maybe he was looking for Patsy, and what turned up was the truth. You did have my parents killed. And he thought he'd killed me for nothing. So he disappeared to collect evidence against you. I'm right, aren't I?"

Clive's crumpled expression told her she was on the money.

"Noel saw me on TV and came to apologize. To find Patsy so we could take you down, but I used that stupid pen. Pens you gave us but hid the fact you'd chipped them. Siobhan said you told her it was for our safety, but that's a lie too. It was to keep tabs on us. A way to find us if we ever did cross you."

"It was for your own good. Don't read more into it than that."

"Then why not tell us they were chipped? We trusted you. Never would have thought to even check them."

She wished she had. Noel might be alive right now.

"You had Foyles kill Noel before he could confirm to me the truth and fill Siobhan in, as well. Because he would have, once he had me to back him up."

"We save lives."

That was the best he could come up with? His only response?

"You used me to eliminate people and steal the evidence that proved you guilty of treason and murder." She had killed innocent people. She could hardly breathe.

"When you showed up at the compound," Patsy said, "I knew Clive had finished collecting the evidence that would incriminate him. He sent you in to retrieve the research and toxin, so I slowed the research, knowing he would bide his time and wait for it, then order a hit on me. Then Hector went to the States. The DEA was coming in and I was afraid. I told you the truth—"

"You left out a good bit, Patsy. You're a traitor to our country. For money."

"I am. And so is he."

Grace was reeling. "He never told me to kill you."

"He would have made up something or he would have sent someone else—like that agent that came for us. Take the research, kill me—or take me in. Guess where Clive takes people like me who can benefit him?"

"Where?"

"Shut up!"

Hollis put a foot on his chest. "You shut up," he barked.

"He puts them away in cells. Private cells where they work for him in labs. Doing what I did for Hector, only for him and for free."

"No," Grace said. But he had said—Siobhan had even said—they had doctors. Grace assumed that meant they knew of doctors, but this information…they literally had them!

"Oh yes. He's threatened me with that plenty. Where do you think I'm going right now? Jail? No."

"I made you rich," Clive said.

"That you did. But you won't be making anyone anything again." She pulled the trigger and ended Clive's life.

Hollis dropped to his knees, grabbed the cuffs and slid them around the wrists of Agent Foyles, who was stirring. "Patsy, give me the gun," Hollis said.

"I did a lot of bad things, Grace. I'm not going to prison."

Before Grace could get to her, the trigger was already pulled and Patsy fell to the floor.

Grace gasped. Hollis took the gun from her and aimed it on the pilot. "Turn us around. Take us to Lander's field and don't try anything." He radioed Cord and told him where to meet them.

Collapsing in the seat, Grace held her head in her hands. Her body ached everywhere. This world was dark. An evil place. Blackmailing. Murder. Bioweapons! Siobhan had the information. They'd have to find her and retrieve it.

When the helicopter landed, they jumped into the water and Cord met them with several deputies. Deputy Jordan wasn't among them.

"Where's Deputy Jordan?" Grace asked.

Cord shook his head. Clive had killed the poor guy.

So much death and destruction. Like this horrible flood that had devastated a town. Clive and his thirst for power and greed had devastated numerous lives.

They took the pilot and Agent Foyles into custody.

Siobhan had vanished. Probably left behind to do cleanup duty. Sweep the place of any evidence they'd been there—it hadn't been on agency time. This had been personal. She couldn't blame Siobhan for following Clive's orders, for lying to her, drugging her or even knocking her out. Clive was a first-class manipulator.

No time to process or even talk to Hollis, they'd gone straight into search-and-rescue mode, helping evacuate those the Coast Guard hadn't gotten to yet. In between rescues, paramedics had checked them out and cleared them. The town was a mess.

Only the most northern tip had been spared. Businesses and residential areas were ruined.

But the rain had let up.

People had been sent to the neighboring towns. Insurance companies were going to have a major payout.

By the end of the day, Grace and Hollis had cleaned up and gotten dry in rented hotel rooms. Tish was safe and across the hall.

A knock came on her door. She opened it to Hollis, looking as bruised and roughed up as she did. "Come in."

He entered her room and sat on the small couch in the sitting room. "How are you?"

"I don't know." She curled up beside him. "No, that's not true. I'm exhausted, Hollis. And I remember being so mad at my dad for not loving me enough, but he did love me. And now I know why it felt like he didn't, and I can't even tell him I'm sorry. I can't start over."

Hollis laid his hand with the broken finger on her knee. "I guess we never know someone's real story or why they behave the way they do. You can't beat yourself up. And you did follow in his footsteps. He'd be proud."

"I killed innocent people."

"You trusted a man who took advantage of you. You thought you were saving lives. It's not the unforgivable sin, Grace. And you know there are people you can talk to."

"Therapy? I'll be in that the rest of my life."

"Nothing wrong with that." He smiled and she carefully laid her hand on his. "What are you going to do next?"

"I have a briefing at Langley. Two weeks from today." She sighed. "I got the call after Cord dealt with the aftermath."

"You don't have to go alone."

Grace looked into Hollis's eyes. "You'd go with me?"

He cupped her tender face with his uninjured hand. "I'd go anywhere with you, Grace. On or off the grid. I love you. Nothing could make me not love you."

Grace's heart swelled. The same kind of love God loved her with. The kind that couldn't separate them. "I love you too, Hollis. You're my favorite."

"You were mine first." He dipped his head and lightly kissed her. They both had split lips and bruised faces. But she felt the unconditional love all the way to her toes.

Hollis paced the lobby waiting on Grace to finish with her hearing at Langley. The day after she regained her memory, the rain stopped. The sun came out. And the people of Cottonwood went to work salvaging their town.

He and Grace had been so overwhelmingly busy helping that they hadn't had much time to talk about their future. Though they had taken the time to update Wilder and the McKnights.

Now, Hollis couldn't deny feeling apprehensive. Grace might want to return to the agency. If she asked Hollis to come with her, he would. He meant it when he said he'd go anywhere with her. But missions could put her on the road and out of pocket for weeks or even months. He was willing to brave it to be with her.

So much so that one evening after they'd returned to their hotel rooms exhausted, he'd slipped out and purchased a spectacular ring. A round solitaire with diamonds encircling it, set in white gold. He was waiting for the right time.

The elevator door opened and Grace stepped off, knocking the breath from his lungs. Dressed in a black pants suit, hair up in a bun. Her bruises were fading and her lip was almost healed. She beamed.

"I'm going to go with—that went well." Hollis hugged her, kissed her on the forehead.

"I told them everything. Agent Foyles—I believe you call him Crewcut—confirmed what I said. But he told a slightly different story. The one Clive manipulated him with. He was the sniper that killed Noel, and he and two other agents who have been brought in confirmed they came after us at the safe house and Foyles also killed Judith Ryland at Clive's command. Another agent killed Deputy Jordan, who was guarding Patsy. I believed him. And Siobhan—she was there. She admitted to murdering Hector's two men, and they were confirmed to be part of his cartel, not mercenaries. Siobhan had lied about knowing it was operatives at the safe house, but she'd been instructed what to say, so I can't fault her for it. With Clive, you didn't question—you just followed orders and trusted him. It was self-defense so she won't be tried for murder. They both thought I'd turned traitorous thanks to Clive, even though Siobhan said she'd had doubts. You don't break Clive's commands, though. I'm cleared."

Relief lifted a weight from Hollis's shoulders.

"And I was asked to take Clive's position. Quite a prestigious one." She smiled.

"Do you want to? Don't let me hold you back. I'd move, Grace."

Grace embraced him and rested her head against his chest. "I know. I love you for it. But no, I don't want this world anymore." She pulled her head back and peered into his eyes. "I want to live in Cottonwood. But there is one thing I need to do. I've been thinking."

"Uh-oh," Hollis teased and she gave him that thousand-watt smile. "The last thought you had was to jump off a moving boat onto a helicopter."

"True. You loved it."

"I'd have loved it more if you weren't in the line of fire." He kissed her nose. "So, what are you thinking?"

"I've lived in a lot of places. I've had a lot of names. But I don't think I've ever been as happy as when I've been Grace. When we leave here, I'm changing my name. I don't want to be Lucy Newark, Valentina Sanchez or even Mad Max."

"That one was growing on me." Hollis chuckled. She was keeping the name he'd given her before she ever even woke from the coma.

"Ha. Ha. Grace Thackery sounds pretty good, right?"

"Almost." Seemed like now was the right time. Where her past, present and future collided. "I love Grace. Thackery…" He turned his nose up and dropped to his knee as he pulled the ring box from his pocket. "How about Grace Montgomery? Would you marry me, Grace? I promise to love you and cherish you and sometimes jump from moving boats with you or shoot leaves hundreds of yards away." He laughed. "I just wanna be with you the rest of our lives." He opened the box and she went slack-jawed.

"Yes!"

Hollis placed the ring on her finger and stood. "I'm going to kiss you now and no matter how many times you might get amnesia...you aren't going to forget this." He claimed her lips and kissed her in a way a woman who knew she belonged to a man ought to be kissed.

Thoroughly.

Tenderly.

Passionately.

• Breathlessly.

When he broke the kiss, she kept her eyes closed and smiled. "I can live with that the rest of my life."

"Grace?"

A woman with blond hair in a red business suit stood nearby.

"Siobhan," Grace said.

"I didn't mean to overhear your conversation... Congratulations. I want to tell you how sorry I am."

Grace held up her hand. "No need. Clive manipulated us all. I would have done the same thing."

"He did. And...I need to make amends. So..." She pointed a few feet away.

A woman who seemed familiar stood with tears in her eyes.

Grace squinted and then slowly shook her head. "No...no, that can't be..."

"It's me, baby. It's Mom."

The woman was familiar because she looked like Grace. Older than in the picture Wheezer had emailed them.

"Mom! I— You— What?" Grace sobbed and her

knees buckled. Her mother fell on her, weeping with her. "Is it really you? How?"

"We were drugged on our flight. I barely remember the pilot strapping me to him before jumping from the plane. When I woke, I was in a glass prison. Your dad—he's gone. Clive promised to keep you unharmed if I worked for him."

"It's true," Siobhan said. "I knew about the research labs. Clive said they were traitors, criminals and instead of prison the government gave them the choice to help in the bioweapons war on terrorism in a covert lab. I believed him. I had no idea they were imprisoned. I had no idea she was your mom. I'd never actually visited the facility. Only Clive had access."

Lucinda Newark held Grace tightly. "I didn't even know you were an agent. He refused to give me any information on you. I wanted a good life for you. And I just got to overhear the sweetest conversation and proposal. Siobhan filled me in on the other things."

Grace stood stunned, but her eyes were lit with joy. Strength. Hope. "Mom, meet Hollister Montgomery. My fiancé. The man of my dreams and my rescuer."

"It's an honor to meet you." He hugged her and thanked God for such gifts.

"And you." She looked at Grace, drinking her in. "You are beautiful." She glanced at her necklace. "You have this! It was going to be a gift from your father on your eighteenth birthday."

"Clive gave it to me—said it was from Dad. I figured it was like a locket but not actually a locket since it won't open. I couldn't bring myself to have it broken or smashed to retrieve what might or might not have been inside."

Lucinda chuckled. "He was a spy through and

through. May I?" She unclasped it from Grace's neck and held it out. Slowly she turned the top clasp to the left…right…left. "There's a little tiny arrow and you can feel the clicks if you can't see it…" The locket popped open. Deep enough to hide a key in, but no key. Only pictures on one side of Grace and her father and the other side was a family photo.

"I remember taking this. I was sixteen." Grace studied the photos. "All this time, you and Dad have been with me. And a piece of his job too. My job. Former job." She wiped a tear. "He loved me."

"Oh, he did. Doted on you. But as you know, the job keeps you moving and keeps you secretive. Often takes you away."

Grace nodded and ran her finger over the photos, then she looked at Hollis. "I'm never going away from you. Or our family." She held up her hand. The diamond sparkled. "You sealed the deal. No take backs."

A family with Grace. "I wouldn't dare. I've seen you with a gun…and a knife…" They walked toward the door, leaving Langley. "And I've seen your fists…seen you squeeze a grown man's neck…"

"All right, Hollister. You made your point. Some days I wish I had amnesia," she teased. "Actually, I wish *you* did."

As they made their way to the street, Hollis pulled her to him. "Grace, I could never forget you. You know why?"

"Why?"

"Because you aren't only in my mind." He placed her hand with the engagement ring on his chest. "You're in my heart."

Hollis never expected to find a woman left for dead on the muddy banks. Never dreamed this moment would come through some of the darkest nights and deepest floods. But here they were and they hadn't drowned. They'd swum their way out with a whole lot of love and mercy.

And grace.

* * * * *

Dear Reader,

I hope you enjoyed this story. I loved writing it. I've always been a big fan of spy movies and novels. What better way to explore amnesia than using a spy who did some things that blurred and even crossed moral lines. But that was Grace's past. Maybe it's your past too. But it's not who you are anymore. In Christ, you are free. You get a clean slate. You get to be a new creation, making new and better choices. No longer are you a slave to sin. And you are forgiven. Completely. Thoroughly. Utterly. No more shame. No more guilt. That's the beauty of salvation. Of mercy. Of forgiveness. Grace finally realized that, and it gave her the liberty to pursue her dream—to love Hollis fully. I pray that if you are battling the same feelings as Grace, you'll take comfort from this story. Cling to truth, and walk in freedom, friend. It's yours.

I love to hear from readers! Please drop me a line and visit me at www.jessicarpatch.com.

Warmly,
*Jessica*

Rookie K-9 officer Lani Branson took in a deep breath as she pedaled her bike along the trail in the Jamaica Bay Wildlife Refuge. Water rushed and receded from the shore just over the dunes. The high-rises of New York City, made hazy from the dusky twilight, were visible across the expanse of water.

She sped up even more.

Tonight was important. This training exercise was an opportunity to prove herself to the other K-9 officers who waited back at the visitors' center with the tracking dogs for her to give the go-ahead. Playing the part of a child lost in the refuge so the dogs could practice tracking her was probably a less-than-desirable duty for the senior officers.

Reaching up to her shoulder, Lani got off her bike and pressed the button on the radio. "I'm in place."

The smooth tenor voice of her supervisor, Chief Noah Jameson, came over the line. "Good—you made it out there in record time."

Up ahead she spotted an object shining in the setting sun. She jogged toward it. A bicycle, not hers, was propped against a tree.

A knot of tension formed at the back of her neck as she turned in a half circle, taking in the area around her. It was possible someone had left the bike behind. Vagrants could have wandered into the area.

She studied the bike a little closer. State-of-the-art and in good condition. Not the kind of bike someone just dumped.

A branch cracked. Her breath caught in her throat. Fear caused her heartbeat to drum in her ears.

"NYPD." She hadn't worn her gun for this exercise. Her eyes scanned all around her, searching for movement and color. "You need to show yourself."

Seconds ticked by. Her heart pounded.

Someone else was out here.

*Don't miss*
Courage Under Fire *by Sharon Dunn,*
*available October 2019 wherever*
Love Inspired® Suspense *books and ebooks are sold.*

www.LoveInspired.com